# ILLEGAL CONTACT

## EMILY SILVER

TRAVELIN' HOOSIER BOOKS

## ILLEGAL CONTACT

Definition: a defensive player interfering with an offensive receiving player more than 5 yards from the line of scrimmage; Making significant contact with a receiver after the receiver has advanced five yards beyond the line of scrimmage.

"Holy shit."

The Mountain Lion emblem stares down at me from across the locker room. The bag I'm carrying cuts into my palm as I squeeze it tighter.

I can't believe it's finally here. The day I've been dreaming about since I started playing peewee football.

My very first day in the NFL.

And playing for the best team in the league.

"Hey man, you doing okay?" Someone claps me on the shoulder as I spin around to look at the beast of a man next to me. "You look a little green around the gills. First day?"

I swallow down the nerves that are threatening to explode. "Is it that obvious?"

This guy is huge. With arms the size of my head, he could knock me flat on my ass with one poke of his finger.

"Matthew Roberts."

I take his extended hand in mine. "I know. Only the best linebacker in the league. Knox Fisher."

He gives me a grin. "And you're the guy that's going to be gunning for my position."

I shrug a shoulder. "I don't know if I'll ever be at your level."

"That's why you learn from the best, just like I did."

Guys start filtering into the locker room. Alex Young, Denver's newest starting quarterback, nods at me.

It's not like me to be starstruck, but holy shit.

Everyone is saying he'll take Denver to a Super Bowl this year. I can't imagine getting to play in one as a rookie. Not that I'll be starting with Roberts in the lineup.

Roberts nudges me, pointing me toward a few free lockers. "Defense is over here. Go ahead and get yourself set up and then I can run some plays with you if you want before practice gets started."

"Really?"

"Really. Trust me, I didn't get to where I am now by myself. Learn from those smarter than you and you'll go far."

"Hey, thanks, man. I really appreciate it."

"No problem. See you out there." He walks off toward his locker. I set my own bag down and take a few deep breaths. This tiny space of wood could be my home for the next however many years.

But I try not to think about that.

The energy is palpable as guys, both rookies and veterans alike, fill the locker room. Trainers and coaches come and go as I change into my pads and practice jersey.

"Where you from?" Roberts asks as we head outside.

The practice field is even more intimidating than the locker room. Guys are already running drills with the coaches, tackling dummies, or catching passes from the backup quarterback.

Out here is where boys become men. Only fifty-three guys will make the final cut.

I try not to focus on that.

"Michigan."

"Fellow Midwesterner. I'm from Indiana."

I smile back at him. "Would it make me sound like a fan boy if I said I knew that? I have your rookie card from when you started with Denver. Reason why I wanted to play defense."

"Shit, kid. Way to make me feel old. You were probably in diapers when I started playing."

I follow him out toward one of the end zones with tackling dummies. "Nah. You started when I was in junior high."

One meaty hand claps me on the shoulder. With dark hair and dark eyes, he's intimidating. No wonder he's so good against opposing offenses. He makes me want to run in the other direction. "Quit while you're ahead."

"Sure thing."

My gaze goes back to the field in front of me. Stands line one side while the city stretches out on the other.

A few people are gathered across the field.

"Who's the chick?" I nod toward the woman walking our way. With her hat pulled low, it's hard to see her face. But those curves? Shit, I'd like to see what they look like without clothes.

"You mean Frankie?"

It's then I notice the man next to her. Figures someone that attractive is already paired off.

"No, the woman next to him."

Roberts shakes his head as he starts stretching. "You're talking about Frankie."

I shake my head at him. "You sure you can still see there, old man?"

"Watch it, kid."

The look he gives me would send me running on any other day. Except now I'm trying to prove myself to make the team.

"Sorry. I just think we're looking at two different things."

His eyes are calculating before his face lights up. "Hey Frankie!" he yells.

The woman marches over to us, holding out a fist to him. "Roberts. Ready to show these guys what it takes to be a linebacker?"

"Absolutely." He fist bumps Frankie, and then stretches his arm toward me. "Have you met our newest rookie?"

"Frankie?" My voice cracks like a preteen.

The person standing before me pulls her hat off. Honey-brown hair cascades down her shoulders. Brown eyes that look ready for a fight stare back at me as she crosses her arms.

This can't be good.

"Name's Coach Rose to you, kid. Assistant linebackers coach."

*Oh shit.*

This really isn't good.

"Uh, hi." I try to recover, offering her my hand. "Knox Fisher."

Her eyes rove over me. Whatever first impression I made on this woman was not the one I wanted to have. As the assistant coach, I'll be working with her on a daily basis.

"Maybe I'll learn your name if you make the team." She nods to the man next to me. "Roberts. Whip his ass into shape."

Oh shit.

I'll be lucky if I make the cut.

"Gentlemen, take a knee."

Grabbing the cage of my helmet, I pull it off. Sweat drips down my face. It feels like it's hotter than the surface of the sun today, but that's because we've been running drills all morning. Newman, our newest rookie, collapses on the ground beside me.

"Fuck, it's hot. I didn't think Denver was hot." His blond hair is practically black with sweat.

Grabbing the water bottle from the bench, I take a swig and pass it down to him. "Welcome to the big leagues. Better get used to it, kid."

"Damn."

Players move around us, taking a knee as Coach Brooks observes all of us.

"You didn't really think I'd go easy on you since it's family day, right?" A few guys laugh at Coach's joke. Not me. I know better. He expects us to work hard in practice. It's where you earn your keep, he says.

"Things are shaping up nicely. Offense, defense, special teams. It's going to be hard to make cuts this year. We've got a lot of great talent out there, and we're going to have a hell of a run this year."

I look at all the guys around me. Denver traded for some new guys last year and drafted a few more to help bulk up our offense. After the loss to San Diego in the AFC Championship game last year, we need the help. You can feel the bitterness from those of us that played in that game.

It was miserable. We played like a group of school kids and lost to a division rival. It fucking sucked. But at least we didn't lose to Vegas.

"It's a new and different season for us. We have a game in London. There's a lot to look forward to. Until then, enjoy the afternoon with your families and we'll see you all back here for practice tomorrow."

Guys break apart as families start to spill out onto the practice field. Pulling my jersey and pads over my head, I drop them on the ground. My practice tee, now cut up to within an inch of its life, clings to me. Fuck, it feels good to be out of pads.

It's really hotter than a ball sac today.

Newman waves to me as he goes to find his family as I drift over to find Jackson with Tenley.

"Hey Knox!" Tenley goes to wrap me in a hug, but seeing how sweaty I am, waves at me instead. "How's the defense looking this year?"

"Hopefully cleaning up the mistakes from last year."

She brushes my comment off, a smile brightening her face. She might be the happiest person I've ever met. "I know you will."

"How's the little guy?"

As if on cue, Noah wobbles up, Jackson right behind him.

"I think he might be a running back." Jackson looks as

hot as I do. It's been a scorching few weeks of practice. "I don't know how he has so much energy."

Jackson flops down onto his back, Noah doing the same. If Jackson does it, he does it. The kid clearly wants to be just like him. "Probably because he didn't just spend all morning lifting weights then running drills."

"He also naps twice a day," Tenley states. "You'd have that kind of energy if you got to sleep twice a day."

Jackson squints up at us. "Trust me, if we're in bed, there's no napping."

"Dude, you can't say that in front of the baby!" I hiss at him. Tenley only laughs at us.

"He can't understand me. Isn't that right?" Jackson picks him up and swings him in front of him. He lets out the loudest giggle.

"I thought I heard my godson." Colin jogs over, dropping a peck on Tenley's cheek.

"Not your godson," Jackson tells him, sitting up with Noah in his lap.

"Please. The kid loves me." Colin gets down in his face, but Noah gives him a blank look. "He just doesn't recognize me."

"Or he doesn't like you," Jackson teases. Movement behind them catches my eye.

Honey-blonde hair glints in the sun. It has a smile stretching across my lips.

Frankie.

Frankie fucking Rose.

The woman that drives me crazy in so many ways. On and off the field.

She's talking with some of the other defensive coordinators, a clipboard in hand. Frankie is always working.

It's the first long look I've gotten of her. She'd been in and out of meetings for the first few weeks of training camp. No doubt learning the new plays we got at the start of camp.

Fuck, I've missed her.

It was a long offseason this year, having gone out the way we did. Even longer without her.

"Something wrong, Knox?" Tenley asks.

I flit my gaze back to her. "What?"

"You have a face." She waves her finger around in front of me before looking around.

"Noah! Come say hi to Uncle Carter!" Alex breaks Tenley's focus from me and she turns to Alex and Carter, now in our small circle.

Thank fuck. I can't imagine what face I was making.

"How come he's Uncle Carter?" Colin whines. "I just want the kid to like me."

"No one said you couldn't be Uncle Colin. But you can't call him your godson." Jackson hands Noah to Carter who gets the same sappy look on his face with the kid.

My eyes keep going back to Frankie. I don't want them to, but I'm drawn to her. Every move she makes, I'm tracking.

"You could just have one of your own, Colin. They'd love you then," Alex tells him, but he is looking at Carter and Noah like it's the best thing in the world.

"I'm good being Uncle Colin. Besides, I don't know if Waffles would like kids."

Jackson laughs at him as he tugs Tenley down to his side. "Waffles loves him. It's fine if you don't want kids."

"I like my alone time with Peyton." He elbows me in the side. "What about you?"

"Kids? Or alone time with Peyton?" I say it just to rile him up. With the look on his face, I know I hit my mark.

"You're a dick."

"I feel sorry for Noah," Carter says. "Poor kid's first word is going to be a bad one."

"It's what happens when you're around these fools." Alex drops a kiss on Carter's cheek.

"Anyone see Logan?"

"He's showing his family around. He said he'd bring them over later," Jackson says, lying down.

I wave a finger at the rest of the guys. "None of you wanted to show your family around?"

"No," they all say in unison.

"You forget I've been here before," Carter tells me.

"And Peyton works here," Colin reiterates.

"If someone is watching Noah for me, I'm happy to not move at all," Tenley says.

"Okay, then." Shaking hands with Coach Jenkins, Frankie turns, her eyes stopping on mine for a fraction of a second, before she walks across the field toward the stands on the opposite side. They're here for when we host fan days, but today, they are blissfully empty.

"I need some water. Be right back."

One of the guys calls after me, but I ignore them. Keeping Frankie in my sights, I walk on the opposite side of the field as she ducks under the bleachers heading toward the equipment shed.

I close the distance to her in a quick jog, grabbing the door so she can't go inside.

"Holy shit, Knox. What are you doing?" Her cheeks are sun-kissed and freckles dot her face. It's fucking adorable.

"You nodded at me."

"I didn't nod at you."

"Yes you did. After you shook hands with Coach Jenkins."

Frankie glances both ways, checking that the coast is

clear, before taking a step closer to me. She's at eye level with me.

"You know we can't be seen together here. Too many eyes."

This is why I love the start of football season so much. Not because it's the game I love more than anything in the world. But because of this woman.

"No one saw me."

"Knox…" her voice trails off.

I take a step closer to her. "I can't come say hi?"

"Not like this."

"Frankie." I sweep the hair off her neck, letting my hand rest there. Her pulse is leaping under my touch.

I dip my mouth closer to hers. Her eyes drift down to my lips. One hand comes up, fisting in my shirt.

She wants this as much as I do.

And fuck if I'm not ready to take.

After not having her for so long, I crave her. Want to feel every inch of her pressed up against me as we start this thing back up.

My lips are a breath away from hers when a whistle from the field breaks through the lusty fog filling my brain. I jump back like I was burned.

Fuck.

Frankie runs a hand through her hair. "I have to go."

I watch her walk away. Watch her hips sway with each step in those shapeless shorts and the Mountains Lions tank she's wearing.

It does nothing to help the growing problem in my shorts.

Because I know what she looks like underneath them.

Adjusting myself, I walk back out onto the field. The guys are all still cooing over Noah.

"Knox. There you are. I was wondering where you

went." Coach Brooks pops up at my side. "Let's find Coach Rose. A few people want to meet our starting linebackers and their coach."

"I think I just saw her that way." I point in the opposite direction I came from.

"Great. Frankie's going to be taking my spot one day. She's one of the best coaches we've got."

"She is, Coach." I fight the grimace. "Best damn coach I've ever had."

Best damn lover too.

But I don't tell him that.

# Chapter Two

FRANKIE

"Newman. You need to be getting lower. You keep leading with your helmet. It's going to draw a flag every time."

Rookies. They know how to play the game, but need a lot of fine-tuning to get them up to par for the NFL.

"Sorry, Coach Rose."

"Don't be sorry. Show me you can do it. Hit 'em hard, hit 'em clean."

He nods at me as he walks back over to the line. Knox grabs him and demonstrates the move that I've been working on with him for the last few weeks in training camp.

"Back on the line, boys." I blow my whistle as they all jump into position. "Just like we've been practicing."

Blowing my whistle again, I watch them start to move. This time, Newman hits the target in the exact spot that I've been reiterating to him.

"Great job, kid! Did you feel that? How you can get more power going lower?"

"That felt great, Coach."

"Good." I slap him on the helmet. "Keep doing that and you'll be well on your way to starting."

He takes a swig of water. "You think so?"

Knox comes up from behind him, grabbing his own bottle. "Everyone's gotta start somewhere."

I give Knox a small smile, before turning back to Newman. "It's true. Fisher here didn't start day one."

"Only because the greatest linebacker ever used to play for us," Knox states.

"What was it like playing with Roberts?" Newman asks. "I can't imagine being surrounded by so many great players."

"Soak it up." Knox wipes a muscled arm across his face. Even sweaty from practice, he's sexier than any person has the right to be. It's harder than it should be to drag my gaze away from him. "Learn everything you can from people who know more than you."

"You got it." Newman puts his helmet back on and jogs back onto the practice field.

"You look too happy," Knox comments as he swigs his own water.

I know my smile must be huge, but it's one of the reasons I love coaching so much. "You don't have to be so smug about it."

"Who said I was being smug?" Knox shields his eyes from the sun as he turns to face me. "Just pointing it out."

I cross my arms over my chest and turn to him. "Do you really want to mess with me?"

Knox raises a single eyebrow. "You know I do."

"How does twenty laps around the field sound?"

"I'm good." Knox throws his hands up and walks back onto the field.

"Keep up the funny business and you will." Grabbing the

whistle, I let everyone know it's time to start again. "Alright, boys. First game of the season is against San Diego. They've cleaned up since last season, so you need to be on it."

"Why do we have to play against them?" a voice whines from somewhere on the field. "Couldn't we play Cleveland? They had the worst record."

"Because," I say, turning to my line, "they beat us in the championship game. The league loves this stuff. I want us to go out there and start strong. No one is going to get around my line, you hear me?"

Every linebacker, and the whole of the defensive line, is looking back at me.

The loss in the playoffs last year hurt. All of the coaches watched hours of film, studied everything we could to try and improve this season.

No one wants to go out to a team from their division one game before the Super Bowl.

We want this year to be different.

"Hell yeah, Coach Rose!" Everyone breaks out into cheers, slapping each other on the helmet.

This is why I love the game. Growing up, I watched my brother build bonds with everyone he played with. I was jealous, always wishing I could play. There was no way my mom would've let me.

I started as a water girl in high school and worked my way up. Once I got started in college, I helped my little brother, even though he played a different position.

I knew I loved the game and wanted to be involved in it any way I could.

I always thought I wanted to be a quarterbacks coach. But when I was assigned to help the defensive coordinator in college, I became hooked.

Something about the defense drew me in—the artful

way they pick apart plays to stop the running backs from getting through.

I love it.

"Rose. Coach wants to see you in his office," an aide yells from down the sideline, breaking me from my thoughts.

Knox glances over at me.

Why is it that every time the coach want to see me, I get a pit of dread in my stomach?

"Sure thing." I eye all of my guys. "Turnover and tackle circuits. We'll work on some plays when I get back."

Walking toward the practice building, I take a few steadying breaths and head inside.

Coach Brooks is waiting for me, papers spread out across his desk. "Frankie. Thanks for coming to see me."

"No problem. Everything okay?" I take a seat in front of his desk, the window behind him looking out onto the field and giving the perfect view of everything that's going on during practice.

"Yes and no. I got some unexpected news from Coach Riley."

"What's wrong?" I sit up straighter, the pit of dread falling away.

"He's decided to retire at the end of the season."

"Really?" I can't hide the shock in my voice. "They were tapping him to be the next head coach."

"Trying to give my job away?" Coach's mouth lifts in a playful smile.

"Sorry. I just didn't think he would hang up his whistle anytime soon."

"Well, our loss might be your gain."

"What do you mean?" I push the hopeful feeling down in my stomach.

"Coach Jenkins will move up to be defensive coordinator. We've always known he'd take over the D."

I nod. "Right."

"Which means the linebacker coaching position is up for grabs."

"Am I up for the job?"

Being the assistant, I do a lot of the grunt work. I'm out on the field executing plays that other coaches draw up. I know my way around the game, but I still don't have much say. This would be a huge opportunity for me.

"You are. You're one of the best coaches I've ever had the pleasure of working with, Frankie. Just keep to the straight and narrow, and the position is all but yours."

I swallow down the guilt that has pushed its way up.

Straight and narrow.

Everything I do for this position is on the straight and narrow.

Except those extracurricular activities. If anyone on the team knew about them, I'd be fired.

And now that I'm up for this promotion?

It makes what we're doing even harder. It'll mean we have to be extra careful. Because I'm now one step closer to my ultimate goal.

I paste a smile on my face, not letting my emotions betray me.

"I won't let you down, Coach."

# Chapter Three

## FRANKIE

"Look what the cat dragged in!" Becky's voice booms across the small bar.

I shake my head, walking through the packed tables to meet my best friend.

"You act like I haven't seen you in months."

She flips her auburn hair over her shoulder, handing me a copper mug. "At least a few weeks. You're already in football mode."

I take a long drink, loving the taste of ginger as it explodes on my tongue. "It's only training camp. I'm not in football mode."

"I feel like a football wife, losing you when the season starts," Becky states.

"I think that's a bit dramatic."

Becky drags a finger through the salt on her glass and sucks it into her mouth. "Dramatic? Probably. But you can't lie and say I see you as much during the season."

"You know I always make time for you, Beck."

"Sure, fine."

"Maybe you don't want to hear my news then."

That has her straightening in her seat. "What news?"

"Our defensive coordinator is retiring at the end of the season."

Her eyes go wide. "What does that mean for you?"

"It means I could be promoted to linebackers coach."

"Oh." She slumps down in her seat. "I thought you'd be promoted to defensive coordinator."

"I have to pay my dues," I tell her as a plate of nachos is set down on the table. "God, I'm starving."

"I think your dues have been paid."

"You forget,"—I grab a chip, heaping with cheese, meat, and guacamole, and shove it into my mouth—"I'm a woman working in a man's world. It'll take me years longer to get promoted."

"Then maybe you should focus on why you're not dating anyone instead of the coaching position." She waves a hand in front of me as she takes a much more ladylike bite. Becky is the only person who can steer the conversation from my promotion to dating with such ease. It's one of the many reasons I love her.

I smile around the bite in my mouth. "You sound like my mother."

She shrugs a shoulder. "You're not getting any younger."

"Did she put you up to this?" I take a sip of my drink. "You know I'm not looking to date anyone. I want to focus on my promotion."

"It doesn't mean you can't do both. You're thirty-five. What thirty-five-year-old isn't looking to settle down?"

I've known Becky since college. We were roommates freshman year and have been friends ever since. While Becky found her own husband at the ripe old age of twenty-one, football has been my focus. Much to her dismay.

"I hate to break it to you, but most men don't want to date someone who knows more about football than they do."

She waves me off. "Those aren't the kind of men you want to date."

Grabbing another chip, I bite off a piece and swallow. "I'm sure you have someone in mind for me?"

"What makes you say that?" she asks innocently.

"Don't think I don't know what you're trying to do."

"Is it really so wrong that I want to go out on double dates with my bestie?"

"If you're trying to force it, yes."

"This guy doesn't even like football. You don't have to worry about his ego."

I cringe at her words. "And why would you think that someone who doesn't like football would be good for me?"

I wave my hand at the passing waiter and order another drink before gulping the rest of my current one down. I'm going to need it to get through this night.

"He's cute. He's our accountant at work. He likes dogs."

"I have to give you an A for effort. But really, Becky, I'm fine."

Her blue eyes are fierce as she pins them on me. "Football isn't going to keep you warm at night."

Maybe not, but a certain dark-haired, tattooed linebacker will.

"What's that face for?" Becky swirls a perfectly manicured nail in my face.

"What face?"

Shit. My cheeks heat as I reach for my drink.

"Like you have something you don't want me to know."

I take a sip, but it's only ice that rattles around. "There's nothing to tell. I'm excited the season is starting."

Becky squints, leaning closer to me. Her studious look has my skin feeling too tight. I don't like being under her watchful stare.

"Seriously. Something's up. You're always happy when the season starts, so I don't know why you're blushing like a schoolgirl who saw her first penis." Her eyes light up. "Did you finally see your first penis? What a big day for my little Francesca."

I throw my head back in laughter. "Good lord, Becky. Say that any louder and the entire bar would hear you."

"You're a football coach. I've only assumed you've seen them in locker rooms." She takes a casual sip of her drink like this is the most normal thing in the world.

"Of course I've seen a penis before," I whisper-hiss at her. No point in letting the entire bar know.

She boops me on the nose. "It's okay if you haven't. I just thought you'd be ogling all those sexy footballers of yours all day."

"They aren't my football players." I shudder. "Besides, I don't spend that much time in the locker room. I have my own office."

"You've never dreamed of one of them taking you in the shower?"

"Now I'm starting to wonder about you. Clearly your sex life needs to be spiced up if you're dreaming about football players in the shower."

She raises a brow in my direction. "At least one of us is having sex on the regular. And I know which one of us it is."

It's hard to argue with her without giving myself away.

Because it's the reason I love the start of football

season. I'm surrounded by football all day, every day. It's nothing new. It's what I love most in the world.

Now, besides the new season bringing a fresh chance at making it to the Super Bowl, it's more.

Stolen nights.

Hidden touches.

Secret glances.

If anyone ever found out, then forget the promotion. I'd lose my job.

Every season, I tell myself it will be the last. We can't keep doing this. That I'll let Becky set me up with someone who isn't the same age as my younger brother.

But the growing heat inside me reminds me why we keep doing this. And even if we could stop, I wouldn't want to.

Because I can't resist Knox Fisher.

# Chapter Four

KNOX

"Hey Grandma."

"Knox, my sweet boy. I'm so glad I caught you."

"I always pick up for you."

"Aren't you sweet. Listen, I want to talk to you about the event next week."

I pace outside the bar. With the season kicking off this weekend, it's time for our annual tradition. One that we've thankfully moved back to our old stomping ground.

"Don't worry, I plan on being there."

"I know that. But I just wanted to see if you wanted to have dinner with me after."

"Doesn't it start at six?"

"Are you implying I'm old by telling me I can't eat late?"

I laugh. "Of course not. But how about we make it before? I'll need to get home because practice is early on Thursdays."

"Before," she huffs. "You'd think you're eighty-seven

and not me. Do I need to teach you how to have fun, Knox?"

"Grandma, I'm fine. I promise. You know how grueling the season gets."

Grueling, yes. Seventeen regular-season games are a lot to put your body through.

Thankfully, I have my own source of relief.

"Fine. I guess I'll let you get away with that excuse."

"Listen, I have to go. I'm meeting the guys."

"Tell them all I said hi. I expect to see Colin next week."

"It's weird how much you two like each other."

She scoffs. "I'm a very lovable person, dear."

"I never said you weren't." I laugh.

"Good. Now, go have fun and play well on Sunday."

I smile at her words. No matter what level I'm playing at, she always tells me that. It's almost like my good luck charm before every game.

"I will. Love you."

"Love you."

"Knox!" Logan shouts my name from the corner as I swing open the door.

"Hey man."

Our group is easy to spot in the bar. Four bigger than average guys stand out.

"You know, I'm surprised you guys wanted to come back to the bar," Logan states. I slide into the open seat next to him.

"We were all told to leave the house tonight. Peyton wanted to have Tenley over for a girls' night," Jackson says, sitting across from me, bourbon already in hand.

It's hard to believe that the season is finally here. Training camp was a whirlwind. Preseason went by in the blink of an eye with most of the starting lineup sitting.

"It's much nicer being in the comfort of my own house," Colin grumbles.

"Yes, coming out in public must be so difficult for you." I wave down the waiter and order more drinks for the table. "You're worse than my grandma."

"Hey!" Colin snaps, pointing a finger at me. "Just because I like being at home doesn't mean I'm like Darlene."

"Dude, she goes out more than you now." I laugh. Our waiter appears, setting down full glasses in front of everyone.

"She gets more action than you," Logan pipes up.

I grind my jaw, debating if taking out our now starting running back would be good for the team.

"Ooh, Knox looks like he is going to kill you," Colin says.

"I'd backtrack out of that one if I were you," Alex whispers to him. "He looks pissed."

I gulp down half my drink. "Maybe I'll just take it out on him in practice."

Logan goes ghostly pale. "I was just joking."

"And I wasn't."

"Moving on from destroying our fellow teammates…" Alex steers the conversation away from the topic at hand. "Do you want to hear my news?"

Colin waves him off. "You're happily married and paired off like most of us here. What other news do you have to share?"

Alex gets a goofy grin on his face. After the year Alex had, the fact that we can joke about this is huge. I can't imagine what he went through all those years. Now he's happily married to the coach's son.

"What is Carter up to tonight?" Colin asks. "He turned down Peyton's invitation to hang out."

Alex shakes his head. "Hence why it became girls' night. He has math club tonight."

"Who would've thought that you'd be dating the coach's son?" I say.

"Married," he corrects me. "You'd think it'd get me out of wind sprints, but no such luck."

"I was ready to puke last week. How I'm not used to them by now, I don't know." Jackson shakes his head.

"Can we get back to my news, please?" Alex interrupts.

"Sorry. Oh captain of ours, share the information you seem to be bursting at the seams to tell us," Colin jests.

Alex rolls his eyes, but we all give him our full attention. "Maybe I won't tell you that Carter and I are starting the surrogacy process then."

"Dibs on godfather!" Colin shouts before I can even process what he's said.

"Wait, really?" I ask, holding out a hand to shut Colin up. "You just got married."

Alex nods. "It can take at least six months to find a match. Carter knows someone at work who did it and has a person, but yeah, we don't want to wait."

"Jackson's dad vibes must be rubbing off on everyone," Logan says.

"You won't hear any argument from me," he says. "Being a dad is the best fucking thing ever. Except of course when he runs into things and starts crying."

"Aww, so you're going to be a dad to Logan then," I laugh.

"Hey! Fuck you—I'm a fully grown adult!" Logan shouts, earning the stares of people around us.

"And this is why it's better that we moved this to the 'burbs." Colin is shaking his head. "No one wanting to throw us out of here because Logan can't behave himself."

"I'm more of a grown-up than you are," he fires back.

"I hope your kids are better behaved than these guys," Jackson says. "You can't take them anywhere."

Alex smiles. "As long as they're healthy, I'm happy."

"Spoken like a true parent. Congrats, man." I clink my glass against his. "Does this mean we're opening up our tradition to more people?"

Jackson rolls his eyes. "I brought Noah once. Get over it."

I throw my hands up in defense. "I wasn't saying that. But if everyone starts popping out babies, it's inevitable that there'll be kids at these events."

"Waffles doesn't cause this much trouble," Colin states matter-of-factly.

"He's a dog, Colin," Alex points out. "You've trained him to behave well."

"Just because Peyton and I don't want kids, doesn't mean he's not like my son. I love him more than any of you fools." He rolls his eyes at us.

"How did we get so off topic?" Jackson asks. "I, for one, am happy for you, Alex. There's nothing better than being a parent. When they look at you like you hung the moon…"

"I'm happy for you, Alex," I tell him. "You guys deserve it."

His eyes gloss over. "I know it's going to be a long process, but I can't wait. It's all I've ever wanted. And to get to do it with Carter? He's going to be a great dad."

"Before you know it, this is going to be a family event," Jackson states. "We just need to find Knox someone."

"I'm happily single."

Except it's the furthest thing from the truth. The one person I want to be with, I can't. If someone finds out, it's the end of Frankie's career. Me? I'd probably get a slap on the wrist and that's it.

Frankie has bigger aspirations than I do. I don't know what life after football holds for me, but I know I don't want to be a coach. And the fact that what we're doing could jeopardize that for her?

It's always there in the back of my mind.

Except I could never deny myself of her.

Of her curves.

Of her smile.

Of the way she gives me shit.

I want all of it.

"You'll eventually find someone, Knox," Logan says, pulling my thoughts away from Frankie.

"Sure." I smile at him, finishing the rest of my drink. The burn of the bourbon helps push aside the melancholy of my thoughts. Flagging down the waiter, I get another.

"If not, I'll make sure Darlene is on it." Colin tips his glass in my direction.

"Don't you have a toast to make, Alex?" I deflect Colin's comment. The sooner I can stop thinking about Frankie, the better.

"Someone doesn't like being in the hot seat," Jackson quips.

Alex waves him off. "I'll give you a break."

I nod in thanks.

"Now, for the annual toast."

Five glasses are raised to the center of the table. Our attention is now fixed on Alex.

"I'm not going to lie, last year was rough. Losing to San Diego the way we did wasn't easy. I know a big part of that was me. I didn't play my best—"

"None of us played our best," Jackson cuts him off. "I

missed an easy field goal that would have pushed the momentum in our favor."

"And if I didn't drop those catches, they would've been easy touchdowns," Colin agrees.

"None of us played our best, Alex," I tell him. "It wasn't just you. It was all of us."

A flush creeps up Alex's neck at our words.

"No one here is going to let you take the blame," Logan says. Even though he didn't play much in the game, he doesn't pass it off on us. "Win as a team, lose as a team."

"Regardless, we have to put the past behind us. As much as we all hated losing to San Diego, we have to look forward." Alex eyes each and every one of us, our disbelief written all over our faces. "I know, I know. They are terrible, but it's not like we lost to Vegas. If we want to be our best this year, we have to move on."

"Easier said than done when we play them twice a year," Jackson grumbles.

"We will," Alex continues, "and we are going to play some of our best football this year. We're going to show the world that the Mountain Lions aren't only the best team during the regular season, but during the playoffs too. This is our time. Drown out the noise of everyone saying we're not good enough. We are. We're going to do the damn thing this year. We're going all the way. I can feel it."

Alex raises his glass higher. "Win as a team, lose as team. We're a family, and there is no one else who I would rather be fighting alongside than you."

We all look around the table. Alex is right. Over the last few years, we've all become a family. You can't go through the things we've gone through and not become close. Each one of these men is like a brother to me. Ones I'd go through fire for.

"To each one of you. To our fellow teammates. To all of our coaches. Leave it all out on the field. Give this season everything you have. I've got your back, just like each and every one of us. To the Mountain Lions!"

"To the Mountain Lions!"

# Chapter Five

KNOX

"**H**ow's San Diego's offense looking?" Alex asks, dropping into the chair next to me.

I shrug a shoulder. We're holed away in a bland hotel conference room to study film. "Their offensive line is weak. They traded away too much talent. If we can take advantage of the holes, it's going to be a long day for them."

"You know,"—Colin points a finger at me, looking up from his own iPad—"you still sound cocky saying that when trying to make it sound like it's their problem."

"I don't want to jinx us. If we don't get a few forced fumbles, I'm going to be pissed."

"That's more like it," Jackson says, coming into the room. He tosses water bottles to each one of us.

"How's Tenley doing?" Alex asks.

"Exhausted. Noah has a fever and isn't sleeping well." Jackson looks exhausted too. I can't imagine trying to be a parent and dealing with our travel schedule.

"Are you sure this is what you want, Alex?" Colin asks. "Sick kids and no sleep?"

He nods his head. "Yes. And it might happen even sooner than we thought."

I set my iPad down on the table and kick my legs up onto the long table. "Everything go well with the surrogate?"

"Yup. Should be able to start the process in the next few weeks. Who knows? At this time next year, we might have a baby."

Colin raps his knuckles on the table. "Dude! Don't jinx it."

Jackson shakes his head at him. "There's no jinxing a baby. They will come whenever they want and you'll love them when they do."

"Exactly," Alex agrees.

"Knox." Frankie's head pops into the conference room. "I need to run over a few plays with you for the game tomorrow. San Diego has made a few changes to their starting lineup and I want to be sure you're ready."

I roll my eyes. "What do you think we're doing in here right now? Braiding each other's hair?"

I don't miss the flash of amusement in her eyes. "Good. Then you won't mind coming with me."

She's out the door before I can fire off another comeback.

"When are you going to learn not to piss off the coaches?" Alex groans. "Especially Coach Rose."

"She's had it out for me since day one." We still laugh at that. But that's not something I'm going to tell these guys.

"Well, maybe if you show her the respect you show the other coaches, you wouldn't have so many extra wind sprints to do." Jackson shudders. "I don't know how you can do that many and not puke."

I slap him on the shoulder as I leave the room.

"Because I have to do so many, that's why. Now, if you'll excuse me, I have some practice to do."

I don't look back as I head out of the room toward the elevator. It's close to curfew, so the halls are empty of football players as I step into the mirrored car and press the button to Frankie's floor. Jazz music filters through the speakers as the doors open. I make quick work of closing the distance to her door.

Checking to make sure the coast is clear, I knock on her door. It cracks open and I slip inside.

"You know you don't have to be such an ass to me, right?" Frankie says before my lips are crashing against hers. The way we each fight to control our kisses always gets me going. Neither one of us likes to relinquish control.

It's what makes the sex so damn good.

And fuck, has it been way too long since I've been with her. This woman drives me crazy.

Most guys look forward to the offseason.

Not me.

Frankie put strict rules into place when we started this thing. There'd be no reason we would be together in the offseason, she said, so how would we explain it if we're seen together? With her position, she has more at stake.

I get it. But lately, it's not enough.

I want more than just hooking up during the season with her. A night here or there. I don't know if I could ever get enough time with her.

I lift her into my arms and move inside the room. The room is the same as every other hotel room we've been in together. Drab curtains and bedspread and a picture of the city above the bed.

Fisting my hand in her hair, I deepen the kiss. Each stroke of her tongue against mine has my cock hardening in my sweats.

Fuck. I love what this woman does to me. She gets me going in no time at all.

Her lips are swollen as I pull back. "If I was nice, they'd think something was up."

The smile that splits her face is menacing. "Would it be bad if I said I liked it?"

Dropping her on the bed, I watch as she bounces toward the center. I press myself over her, letting her feel every hard inch. "You get off on it, you'd say?" I drag my nose up the slope of her neck, inhaling that sweet scent of hers.

Frankie is a conundrum.

Hard and soft at the same time.

Athletic yet feminine.

A woman in an old boys' club world.

She somehow makes it work.

"You know I do, Knox." Cupping my cheek, she brings my face up to hers and takes another kiss.

I let her have control this time, flipping us over so she's on top of me. I rock into her and she moves over top.

God, it's been so long that I could blow my load now.

Soft hands roam over my chest, slipping under the hem of my shirt. Delicate fingers trail over the hard ridges of my abs.

"Someone's been working out this offseason." Frankie's pupils are blown wide as she sits back on me. Pushing up off the bed, I yank the T-shirt over my head and shamelessly flex my abs.

"Gotta keep up with the rookies."

Frankie drinks me in. "And some new tattoos, I see."

Her fingers trace the new ink on my left pec. I like that she notices these things. Dipping down, her tongue traces the Vitruvian Man.

"Fuck, Frankie."

I can feel her smile against me. "You like that?"

"You know I do."

I move her under me. Those soft strands of her hair spread out across the pillow. She's a fucking angel.

I'll never get my fill of looking at her. Deep brown eyes that only I can seem to read. A smile that doesn't show her true feelings when out on the field.

How am I the lucky bastard that gets to see her like this?

My hands find her shirt and pull it off her. Her chest is flush, tits heaving, as I pull one cup down and take a diamond hard nipple into my mouth.

"Mmm. I've missed your mouth."

"Oh you have, have you?" I flick her nipple with my tongue. I savor, I suck, I take my damn time, because I don't give a fuck right now if it's close to curfew.

I want Frankie.

Frankie smacks me on the ass. "I don't know why."

"I can give you a few reasons if you need reminding."

I kiss my way down her soft stomach, fingers trailing in their wake. She squirms under me as I pull the waistband of her shorts down and over her ankles.

"And has your pussy missed me too?" I drag a finger through the wet spot on her underwear.

Fuck. I love that I do this to her.

"You're really asking me that?"

I smile as I push her legs apart. "I'm not asking you that."

"I don't know why I put up with you." Frankie throws an arm over her eyes.

"I think you know why." I drag my tongue over the fabric of her underwear. More squirming.

"If you didn't give me such good orgasms…"

It's more than that, but right now, I don't care. Because I'm ready to give her one fucking amazing orgasm.

It's been too long. So long, that I almost forget what she looks like when she comes.

*Almost.*

"Just good? Tsk tsk, Frankie. It must be time to step up my game."

"That's not a challenge."

I peer up her body to find her eyes locked on mine.

"Oh, I think it is." Crawling up her, I take her lips in a heated kiss.

She nips and sucks at my bottom lip, eliciting a growl from me. My hands relearn the curves of her body that I've missed so much during the offseason while hers trace down my back and into my sweats.

Each squeeze of her hands pulls me farther into her. The need between us is palpable, a living, breathing thing.

"I need to feel you inside me, Knox." Her voice is laced with lust.

"Not yet."

Standing, I strip out of the rest of my clothes. My dick is hard as I give it a slow stroke. Frankie looks downright defiled with one tit popping out of her bra and her underwear still on.

"Then why are you just standing there?" Frankie reaches behind her and pops her bra off, flinging it at me.

Taking a step closer, I press one knee onto the bed. Her hand reaches out to cover my own while my free hand does its own exploring.

She takes over stroking me while I press one finger inside of her.

"God, that feels good." Frankie's hand stutters as I move in and out of her.

"I can say the same to you." I thrust into her tight fist, precum leaking from my dick.

"Mmm." Frankie closes her eyes, throwing her head back as her moves start to falter. She's getting close, her pussy fluttering around my finger.

"Are you going to come for me?" I lean down over her, our lips touching but not kissing.

"Yes."

I stop, pulling my finger almost all the way out. Fisting a hand in her hair, I tilt her head back. Brown eyes widen in shock. "Let me hear you ask nicely."

She bites down on her lip, giving me a coy look.

Fuck, is that ever sexy.

"Please, Knox?"

"Please what?" I push my finger inside just a bit more.

Frankie squeezes my dick. Damn. She's good.

"Please make me come." She bats those thick eyelashes up at me.

"Your wish is my command." I take her lips in a searing kiss as I push two fingers inside of her. I swallow each gasp. My thumb finds her clit. The smallest brush has her starting to convulse around me.

"Yes!" She tears her lips away. "Oh God, yes!" Her shouts echo across the quiet room as my fingers pulse in and out of her as she comes down from her high. Her grip on me has loosened enough that I pull out.

Frankie looks blissed out of her mind, skin flushed from her orgasm, pussy still wet from her release.

"You're the sexiest fucking woman on the planet, do you know that?" I cover her body with mine, intertwining our fingers as I kiss her. I don't give her much time to recover, dragging my leaking cock through her wet folds.

"Why don't you show me?" Frankie's lips travel down my neck, sucking on the beating pulse in my neck.

"Negative tests?" I ask.

She nods. "You?"

"Negative. Birth control?"

"Still on it."

Lining myself up with her, I sink inside.

*Fuuuuck.*

There is nothing better than being bare inside of her. We haven't used condoms for a long time now. It's only been Frankie for a long time. No one else compares to her.

"I forget how big you are sometimes," Frankie whispers more to herself.

I smile. She stretches tight around me as I bury myself inside her. "Fuck, you feel so good."

I kiss her shoulder. Her neck. Her jaw. Anywhere I can find as I let her adjust to me. It gives me a moment to calm down. I don't want to blow my load the minute I'm inside her after all these months.

"You ready?" I whisper into her ear.

Rocking her hips up, she takes me that much deeper. "Yes."

"Then hold on."

Finding her eyes, I drag my long length out of her before thrusting inside. I give a few steady pumps before I hike one of her legs up on my hip for purchase.

"Right there." Frankie's words are muffled as her body moves in time with mine. She meets me thrust for thrust. Her nails dig into my back, ratcheting my pleasure higher and higher.

"You need to come," I bite out. Fuck, I'm so close. I don't want to come before she does.

Her eyes, bright with desire, spark up at me. "Do I need permission?"

"Fuck, Frankie. If you don't come right now, I'm going to lose my mind."

Wrapping her arms around me, she pulls me all the way down on top of her. Her nipples brush my chest, and it pushes me that much closer to the edge.

I reach between us and find her clit. A few strokes has her clamping down on my cock as she starts to come again.

Fucking finally.

I capture each moan as I pump harder. Sweat trickles down my back as I push into her again, coming apart at her touch.

"Fuck." I throw my head back, neck muscles straining as I pour my release into her. Her legs hold me to her as I collapse my weight on her.

"I forgot how good that feels." Frankie drags a finger down my spine.

"You're telling me." I kiss her chest, not bothering to move. I don't want to leave her warmth yet.

This right here is one of the reasons I look forward to football season so much. Don't get me wrong; I love the game. I love picking apart opposing offenses and sealing a hard-won game for our team.

Being with Frankie?

Fuck, she's the best damn thing about football.

And I'll take our secret to the grave.

# Chapter Six

## KNOX

**M**usic pulses through me as I walk into the locker room, the guys all around me. I'm in the zone. I've been working hard. Not only in the training room, but studying film. Heading into my seventh year in the league, I have something to prove.

Last year was hard. We lost to San Diego in the championship game. Everyone blamed themselves, but I didn't play my best. I had some missed hits and some dumb penalties that didn't help.

I'm hungry.

To get so close, to have the Super Bowl within arm's reach, and not make it? It was the worst kind of failure.

And I don't want to repeat it.

The locker room is already bursting with energy as I head in. Guys are dancing to music I can't hear as I head to my cubby.

The black and yellow of my jersey greets me. It puts a smile on my face. I love seeing my name etched along the back. Pulling it out, I trace the captain's patch on the front. It's a responsibility I've never taken lightly.

Jackson claps me on the shoulder. I yank my head-phones off. "Ready, Knoxy?"

I grin back at him. "You know I am."

"Damn. I'd hate to be San Diego's QB and be on the receiving end of a Fisher Flatline."

"There will be no flatlining anyone today. Good, clean hits only."

I hated the nickname that started after my first big hit when I was a rookie. Sure, it was a legal hit, but it wasn't a pretty one. And so the nickname began.

"It won't be a cakewalk today." Alex drops his bag into his locker beside mine. "San Diego will want to start the year off with a win after losing the Super Bowl. They have even more to prove. They still have a good team with a good defensive line."

"Relax, just having some fun here," Jackson says with a laugh.

"Damn. If Jackson is telling you to relax, then you know something is wrong." Colin wraps his arm around Alex and me.

"I don't know about you, but I want to start the season off strong. Especially after the way we ended last year."

Logan pops up next to us. "It just means it wasn't our time."

"That's very zen of you, rookie." Colin drags his tie over his head, changing out of his required pregame suit and into his workout gear. "When did you come to this decision?"

"Believe me, it wasn't easy. Fixating on it isn't going to help."

"Okay, seriously. This whole vibe from you is freaking me out." Colin grabs him and ruffles his hair. "Who are you and what have you done with Logan Winchester?"

Logan shoves him off, shrugging his shoulders. "My

grandpa wouldn't let me sit around being sad. And then he put me to work."

I laugh. "That's one way to do it. I played a lot of Bingo with my grandma."

"Not that much Bingo," Colin corrects.

Rolling my eyes, I unbutton my suit jacket and hang it up. I strip down and change into my warm-up gear. "No, because Bingo was dubbed too dangerous. Colin certainly didn't help the situation."

He gives me an affronted look. "Me? I wasn't the one throwing Bingo chips! I just caught one in the eye because of it!"

"Because you told them they were cheating!"

Colin follows me out as we head onto the field.

It's the perfect day for football. It's hot and sunny as the stands start filling up. By the time we get to kickoff, the stands are going to be rocking.

"Maybe a little less talking, guys, and a little more warming up?" Frankie is already out on the field with some of the younger guys.

"Sure thing, Coach." I hide the smile as I watch her help the other guys.

Fuck, I love the start of the football season. Not just because of the game, but because of Frankie.

Being with her is quickly becoming addicting. I don't know when the switch flipped, but Frankie is the only woman who can satisfy the growing beast inside me.

I've watched every single one of my brothers-in-arms pair off. They've turned into saps, gushing about the partners in their lives.

Not me.

For the last few years, my dating life has been the subject of mocking from them. Not that it bothered me. I've always had Frankie.

Even if she isn't mine to have.

I go through my standard warm-up, stretching and jogging around the field. I put a little more effort into it, knowing Frankie's eyes are on me. I've always wanted to play better for her.

Autographs are signed for the kids waiting along the tunnel as I head back inside.

The closer we get to kickoff, the more the adrenaline starts to flow.

I live for this feeling. There's nothing better than running out on the field with the crowd chanting your name.

"Alright everyone, it's that time."

Coach's voice brings me back. He's standing in the middle of the locker room. Eager eyes are looking back at him.

"This is the start of a fresh season. Last season didn't end how we wanted it to, but I don't want to focus on that. I only want us to look forward."

Alex and I turn to each other. Both of us carry this loss harder than most. I know the coach is talking directly to us with those words.

"One game at a time. Focus on your game. That's all you can do. And remember what matters most. We're a family. Drown out the outside noise. Pundits will speculate. Let them. Stand by the men beside you, and we have what it takes to go far."

Coach looks over at me, giving me the nod.

"Alright, boys!" My voice echoes around the quiet locker room. "You heard what coach said. We're a family. Fight for the man next to you. Play your game and we'll go far."

I step into the center of the locker room, throwing my

fist up as everyone gathers around me. "Family on three. One, two, three…"

"Family!" shouts around me as guys start funneling out of the locker room.

The announcer is getting the crowd ready as the cheerleaders file onto the field, ready for the team to run out.

We go through the pregame traditions. The national anthem is sung before we head out to midfield for the coin toss. We win and defer to the second half.

"Great day for some football, boys." Frankie gathers the defense around her as the ball is kicked off. "Hit 'em hard, hit 'em clean."

We all nod at her as we head out onto the field.

"You heard what Coach Rose said. Good clean start. Don't let them get a first down."

San Diego calls the play—a run. The running back doesn't make it two yards before he's being pulled down. They go back to the same play on second down and don't get far.

This time, their QB lines up in the pocket. I'm watching the guard, who's focusing on the defensive backs, allowing me to spin past him after the ball is snapped and get a solid hit on the quarterback.

Loss of seven yards. Fourth down.

The best start to the game we could have asked for.

Frankie's waiting at the sideline as the defense comes off the field.

"Nice job, Fisher. Keep it up."

I nod, grabbing a swig of water. I hide the smile I really want to give her at her words of praise. "Thanks, Coach."

The whole team keeps it up throughout the entire game, leveling San Diego 34-17.

The perfect start to the season.

# Chapter Seven

### FRANKIE

*Calm down, Frankie. There's no need to be nervous.*

It doesn't help. My nerves get the better of me. When the invitation went out to the team about today's event at Knox's grandma's retirement home, I couldn't say no.

I don't get to see Knox outside of football. Ever.

Is it risky, coming here tonight? Yes. But with the entire team being invited, no one should be any wiser.

Turning down another hallway, I find another dead end.

"You look lost. Can I help you?" An older woman greets me as I turn back the way I came.

"Sorry. They told me the community room was this way. I'm looking for the Mountain Lions."

Her face lights up. "Ahh, yes. It's so wonderful they come here." She points me in the direction and walks next to me. "Are you with the team?"

I nod. "I'm an assistant coach."

"Oh." The look of shock that crosses her face is something I'm all too familiar with. Doesn't make it sting any less. "I don't know if I've met a female coach."

I plaster a fake smile on my face.

"Well, you must be good if you're with the Mountain Lions. Everyone is right through there." She gives me a hesitant smile before leaving me.

The community room is loud. Noise bounces around wooden floors. Doors on the side of the room that looks out to the mountains are thrown open to let in the early afternoon air. People are shouting to be overheard as several members of the team are spread out around the room.

I venture in, smiling at the groups of people clustered around the tables.

"Frankie. What are you doing here?"

Knox's voice stops me short. The woman next to Knox smacks him in the chest. Wrinkles line her face, but her smile is bright. Her eyes are the same color as Knox's. "I raised you better than that." She turns her fierce stare from him to me. "Please ignore my grandson. I'm Darlene. I'm glad you could join us."

I shift my eyes from Knox. With the tight black T-shirt that shows off his thick arms and tattoos, it's hard not to pay attention to him.

"Thank you," I address Darlene. "I know some of the other coaches were talking about coming, so I figured I would too."

Darlene loops an arm through mine. "You're one of Knox's coaches?"

I nod. "Assistant coach."

"Doesn't matter, dear." Her face lights up as she pulls me toward the table in the corner. "Why don't you join our group?"

"What are we playing?"

"Dominoes." She states this like it's the worst game out there.

"You don't like dominoes?" I ask, grabbing the plain tin from her.

"Tell her why we can't play bingo, Grandma." Knox flips the tiles over, his fingers ghosting over mine. It sends nerves racing through me. Even the slightest touch of his has the power to turn me into a puddle.

"It's not my fault that nosy Nellie can't win without cheating," Darlene huffs.

"She wasn't cheating if she couldn't see the board," Colin defends, dropping into the seat next to me.

"She saw it enough to know she flipped it over."

"Do I need football gear to play dominoes?" I ask, leaning back in my chair.

Colin gives me a wary look. It has me shifting in my seat. I know Knox hasn't told any of the guys what we're doing, but his studious gaze makes me uncomfortable.

"With this group, you might." Knox leans back in his chair, muscles rippling under. It's like he knows this drives me crazy and I can't do anything about it. "Colin took some bingo chips to the eye."

"It fucking hurt." He points at Knox.

"If you're not careful, Knox Henry, I am going to throw these at you. I don't think your coach here would be too happy with me if you couldn't play on Sunday."

Colin bursts out laughing next to me as I try to hide my smile. Knox sinks back into his chair like a sullen toddler who just got put in time-out.

"Darlene, if you're not careful, you might give Peyton a run for her money." Colin winks at her.

Darlene bats her eyelashes at him. "Oh honey, listen to you sweet-talkin' an old woman."

"For the love of God, stop," Knox groans.

"What?" Colin elbows him. "Don't want to call me grandpa?"

"Frankie, would you bench me on Sunday if I punched Colin here?" He throws his thumb in Colin's direction.

"I think you would get a pass on that one. Can't lose our starting linebacker before the hardest game of the season."

Colin looks offended. "And we can afford to lose our best wide receiver?"

"Wide receivers are a dime a dozen," Knox states. His eyes don't move from mine. No one else would notice the playful glimmer there, but I do.

He's easy to read. He wears his emotions on his sleeve.

"Darlene, are you going to let them talk to me like this?"

"Oh, fuck off, Colin. Just play your domino." Knox waves him off.

Colin flips him off as he plays his tile.

"Sorry to burst your bubble, dear, but you're not who I'd bring home." Darlene plays her own tile.

"Now who would you be bringing home?" Colin leans forward, looking at Darlene like she has the juiciest piece of gossip. "Don't tell me it's another football player."

"Oh no. The world doesn't revolve around football, as much as you three like to believe." She pats Knox on the arm. "Harry Connick Jr. He does it for me with that voice of his. Mm-hmm."

"I thought you were all about Nicolas Cage?" Knox sets his tile on the board.

"Nicolas Cage? Please." She shakes her head and frowns. "I have better taste than that."

Knox looks confused as he throws down another domino. "What do you have against him, Grandma?"

"Have you ever paid attention to any movie he's in?

He's terrible. Thank you, next." She waves him off as she takes her turn.

Knox pushes a hand through his hair before turning his ire on Colin. "I'm blaming you for this."

"What?" He throws his hands up in defense. "It's not like I asked her."

Knox slaps him upside the head. "You absolutely asked her and this *is* your fault."

Darlene turns to me as they continue to bicker. "Are they always like this at practice?"

"Usually, but they're out on the field, so nothing we hear."

"How long have you been coaching, dear?"

"Thirteen years."

"Wow. That's quite the career. Little Knox here would've been a baby when you started."

"Not quite." My laugh is uncomfortable.

It's something I'm always thinking about. It sits there in the back of my mind whenever we're together.

Knox was in high school when I started my coaching career. He couldn't even legally drink when he joined the league, having been drafted at twenty.

*Why can't I find a decent guy my own age?*

"Well, you deserve a medal for dealing with all that testosterone." Darlene clasps my arm, giving it a squeeze. "I don't know how you put up with all of those men."

Her comment derails my wayward thoughts. "And I thought you would like that."

"There is such a thing as too many men."

"What in the world are you two discussing?" Knox interrupts.

"Working with so many men." I rest my elbow on the table, leaning toward Knox. I love how easy he is to rile up around his grandma. The love between the two of them is obvious. It makes me miss my own grandparents.

"If you say a word to encourage her…" Knox glowers at me.

I shift closer to him, giving him my smarmiest smile. "You'll what? Not like you can bench me."

Darlene cackles next to me. "You're delightful, darling. I wish I could say the same for my grandson here. He's about as interesting as an overcooked potato."

"Yeah, stop being a potato, Knox." Colin is giddy.

Knox bangs his head against the table. "I really hate you guys."

"There, there." His grandma pats his back. "Play your tile that I see you have so I can win the game and beat ol' Nellie over there."

Knox shoots up at her words. "Have you been cheating this whole time, Grandma?"

She looks affronted at the accusation. "Why would I ever cheat? It's not my fault I've been able to see your hand the entire time." Darlene leans over to me. "He was never very good at playing games when he was little."

"This is why games get banned here. People cheat and get angry."

"How's everything going over here?" Peyton walks over before Darlene has a chance to fire back at Knox.

"Just peachy," Knox grumbles.

"That potato over there isn't happy because Darlene is cheating." Colin beams up at Peyton.

"Did I miss something?" Peyton smiles down at Colin like he is the only person in the world.

"Knox being cranky. Nothing new." Darlene drops her tiles on the table and stands. "I think I'm going to go play with the girls. Poor Knox has his panties in a twist about losing."

"Grandma," he groans.

She leans down and gives him a kiss on the cheek. "I love you, baby boy. Make sure you listen to Frankie. I don't want to hear about you giving your coaches a hard time."

"This isn't peewee football. How would you hear about it?" He gives her a confused look.

"Frankie here is welcome back anytime."

"I would love to come back, Darlene. Maybe you can teach me how to make sure Knox listens better at practice."

"Ooh. Called out!" Colin laughs.

"Okay. Let's give them a minute." Peyton pulls Colin out of his chair. "Darlene, it was wonderful to see you again. Think you can host another fundraiser in a few weeks?"

"You just tell me when."

Colin leans over and gives her a peck on the cheek. "Darlene. Until next time."

"You keep catching those passes. I want a Super Bowl." She points at him, making sure he hears her words.

"I'll do my best. I don't want to disappoint my biggest fan."

"Darn right."

Peyton and Colin link hands and walk off to another table together, the picture of the happy couple. It makes me wish that Knox and I could do that.

Except that will never be us. We're just filling a need— a need only the two of us can fulfill—during the season. Trying to maintain a relationship on a football schedule isn't easy.

I keep waiting for the day when he tells me he met someone. Someone his own age, who doesn't worry about being caught that they're sleeping together.

It's wrong. So wrong, that sometimes it baffles me why we're still doing this.

"Frankie?" Knox's voice sounds like he's been trying to get my attention.

Shaking off the wayward thoughts, I turn back to Darlene. "It was great meeting you."

"You too. I'll see you next week, Knox."

She kisses him again and we're left alone.

"You okay?" he asks.

"I'm good." The ache that ran through me is still sitting in my chest.

"Want me to walk you out?"

"Sure."

The sun has long since set as a cool breeze blows through the parking lot. I wrap my arms around myself, trying to stave off the cold.

"I'd apologize for my grandma's behavior tonight, but she's always like that." There's a happiness to Knox's words.

"You're lucky to have her. I wish I had family that lived close by."

"She's something, alright." Knox toes at the ground, silence settling around us. "I'm glad you came tonight."

Looking around, I realize we're the only two outside. I give his bicep a quick squeeze. "Me too."

"You know you're going to have to come back now, right?"

"If I didn't, your grandma would just drag me here herself."

Knox smiles at me. The one that makes me weak in the knees. The same one that reminds me that even though this isn't something we should be doing, I'm still going to keep doing it. "You're not wrong."

It's like neither one of us knows what to say next, but

we don't want to leave. It's hard, but I take the first step back.

"Have a good night, Knox."

"See you Saturday night?" he questions, lingering just a moment longer.

"Like always."

Like I could ever refuse him.

# Chapter Eight



"Hey man. Where are you headed?" Logan stops me in the hall on the way to the elevator.

Fuck. I can't really tell him I'm off to meet Frankie. After seeing her earlier this week at my grandma's retirement center, she's been all I can think about.

"Just heading out to take a walk."

"Want to grab a drink with me? The other guys are all moping around together because we're not at home." Logan rolls his eyes, but I know it's because he can't talk to Audrey. Last I heard, she was off in another country training for the World Cup.

"Sure, kid." Slapping him on the shoulder, I steer him into the elevator. "But you know you'd want to be up there just as much as them."

He shoves his hands in his pockets. "Have you ever been in a relationship?"

"Uhh…" I try to come up with an answer for him, one that will hopefully get him off my case.

"Right, sorry. I know you're happy being single. But I

hate that Audrey is halfway around the world and I can't talk to her."

The elevator spits us out into the lobby as Logan bemoans being so far away from his girl. Putting us directly in Frankie's path.

It takes everything I have not to step right back into this elevator and go back up with her. But I can't. Not with Logan at my side.

"Gentlemen. Where are you headed?" Frankie asks, her face not giving anything away.

"Grabbing a drink. Is that allowed?"

I don't miss the bite in Logan's tone. After everything I've told the guys about her, they aren't her biggest fans. It's better that way. Fewer suspicions on us.

"As long as you're ready for tomorrow. Philly is a tough team, so be ready." Frankie looks at Logan before shifting her gaze to me.

The last place I want to be is hanging out with Logan. I'd rather be in bed with the woman in front of me. Being wrapped up in her is just about my favorite place to be.

"They'll be no match for us. We're ready." She rolls her eyes at my wink.

"You better be." Frankie steps into the elevator, a bag swinging by her side. "Or I'll make sure you feel it during practice on Tuesday."

Those words shouldn't be as hot as they are. Because I know the real truth behind them.

It's what comes after practice that I'll like.

"No sweat, Coach Rose."

"I'll see you at the game tomorrow." The doors close on her.

Logan whistles after her. "She really does have it out for you."

I play it up. "I don't know what I ever did. Maybe I'm just too damn good of a football player."

Snorting, Logan finds a high-top in the bar. "Or maybe it's your big head that she likes."

"I'm sure that's it."

"Pretty ballsy for you boys to be venturing out." The server appears at my elbow.

"Let me guess…Philly fan?"

"You can't live in this city and not be cheering for them."

"Nothing new. Tip will be good if you bring us a few beers."

"Good on ya, man." He leaves us be.

"Must be nice making those veteran dollars."

"Hey, you'll be getting a nice contract when your rookie one is up, Winchester."

Two beers in icy pint glasses are dropped off at the table.

"Until then, you're buying." Logan holds his glass up in cheers.

"Maybe this round. You're not hard up either."

Logan laughs. "No. But I'm working on buying a house back home."

"Where's home again?" I ask.

"Dixon, Idaho. Little nowhere town, but I love it."

"You get home often?"

He shakes his head. "Not as often as I want to. Where's home for you?"

"Michigan."

"And your grandma lives here?"

"Oh yeah. Said someone had to keep me in line my rookie year." I laugh, sipping the cold beer.

"I'm sure that's how it goes."

"I don't know if I would have made it through my first

year without her. But then she wanted to be around people her age, so she moved into a retirement community."

"And that's where she gets into trouble," Logan says with a snort.

"I'm sure you have grandparents like her."

Logan waves me off. "I was definitely the troublemaker growing up. Middle of five."

"Damn. I bet that was fun growing up."

"You don't have any brothers and sisters?"

I shake my head. "It was always just my mom and me. We lived with my grandparents for a while, but I never felt like I was missing out. I always had football."

No matter what shit was going on in my life, it was always there for me. It never left me like people did. I could always rely on it. Even through the hard days.

"Some days I wish I had that quiet. But I wouldn't trade it for anything." Logan gulps down the rest of his beer. "You want another?"

I drain the last third of mine. My mind has already drifted to the woman upstairs that I want to see. "No. We should probably get back up. Don't want to get in trouble for missing curfew."

"I want to text Audrey before going to bed."

"Did you say she's in a completely different country? You don't want to wake her up."

"I know, but I can't help it. Some days I feel like she's just keeping me around to boost my ego."

"What in the fuck makes you think that?"

"Dude." Logan slaps me on the arm. "Audrey is a gold medalist. She's older than I am. She could easily find someone way better than me."

"Nah. You play in the NFL. She likes you."

His words plant the seed of doubt. Is that what Frankie

thinks this is? Her boosting my ego? Am I a lost little puppy just following her around?

"Anything else, boys?" The server appears before us.

"Nah. We're good."

"You two will be needing all the sleep you can get, even though there's no way you're going to beat us."

"You wish," Logan tells him. "I'll be tearing down the field tomorrow."

He shakes his head at us as I drop a large bill on the bar. "Thanks, man."

"Thank you." His eyes are wide. "A good tip doesn't mean I'll be cheering for you tomorrow."

"I wouldn't expect it."

He waves as Logan and I head back through the lobby.

"You ready for tomorrow? I know Coach has you alternating with Taylor as starter."

"Fuck. I'm so ready, I can almost taste it." Logan stuffs his hands in his pockets and looks at me with giddiness. "Is this what it felt like before your first start?"

I smile at him, a big, goofy grin painting my face. "Hell yeah. There's no better feeling in the world. I know you'll do great."

I clap him on the shoulder as the elevator opens to our floor. I know Frankie is one above us. My mind works fast as I try to think of how I can bow out. Ever since Logan opened his mouth, doubt has been clawing its way in my head.

"Crap. I left my wallet downstairs. I'll see you tomorrow." I grab around for my wallet, knowing it's tucked securely in my back pocket.

"Sure, no problem. See you on the bus." Logan gives me a small wave as I press the button for Frankie's floor.

This time, the halls are deserted as I close the distance

between me and her door. My knock is soft as I hear the TV mute behind the door.

"What are you doing here?" Frankie hisses, pulling me into the room and shutting the door behind me. "I said I'd see you at the game tomorrow."

"I thought that was just a way to get rid of us."

The glow of the hotel room casts Frankie in a different light. Instead of the usual khakis, polo shirt, and hair pulled back tightly, soft waves fall down around her face. The dress she's wearing clings to her curves, dipping low between her tits. Brightly painted toes stick out from the bottom. This image of her is messing with my head.

"Knox, my period started this morning. The last thing I want to do is screw around with you."

I take a step back.

She smacks me on the chest and turns back into the room. Said dress is swinging around her in a blur of color. "Don't be a Neanderthal, Knox. Women have periods."

"Sorry." I shake my head out of the stupor. "Do you need anything?"

"I'm not in the mood, Knox."

"I wasn't—"

Frankie doesn't let me finish, spinning on her heel and coming at me. "I said I'm not in the mood to screw around. I have cramps from hell, so if you want to watch romantic comedies with me and eat ice cream, you can stay. Otherwise you can go jack off in your room."

I grab the finger poking me in the chest. "Hey. I wasn't asking for that."

"Really?" Frankie drops a hand on her hip, giving me the fierce look that sends my teammates running in the opposite direction during practice.

"Did I come here for that? Yes, I won't lie. You know that. But I'm not a Neanderthal."

"Prove me wrong."

Dropping her hand, I toe off my tennis shoes and flop down on the bed. Grabbing the phone, I dial the number for room service.

"What are you doing?"

I hold up a finger as a man picks up on the other line. "Hi. Can I please get some mint chocolate chip ice cream sent up? Enough for two people."

"Right away. Anything else?"

Covering the receiver, I look over to Frankie, arms crossed in front of her chest. "You want anything else?"

Frankie's lip quivers. "Ice cream is good."

"We're fine. Thanks." I hang up the phone and hold my hand out to the woman standing in front of me. "So, what movie are we watching?"

"Are you really planning on staying?"

Frankie hops over me and situates herself next to me. Our sides are touching, all the way from shoulders to toes. Warmth fills my entire body from the innocent touch.

"Of course I am. Ice cream and hanging out with you. Now,"—I pin her with a look—"what movie are we watching?"

"*What A Girl Wants.*" Frankie reaches across me and grabs the remote, unpausing the TV.

The movie plays while we wait for room service. The farther into the story we get, the more confused I am.

"Wait, how did she just jet off to London like that? She's eighteen."

Frankie laughs next to me. "It's a movie, Knox. Don't ask these questions."

"But how is this believable?" I throw a hand at the TV. "No one would believe this."

"It's an escape for a reason." Frankie drags my arm down, holding it tight. "Just watch."

A knock on the door has Frankie popping up next to me.

"Let me get it." I go to stop her, but she's already on her way to the door.

"It's my room. Let me."

Her voice carries into the room as she pushes a cart inside. Grabbing two bowls, she takes the lids off and brings them over to the bed.

"How'd you know I like mint chip, anyway?" She buries the spoon in the thick green ice cream and takes a bite.

"Because I know you."

I mimic her, taking a bite.

"I guess you do." She drags the spoon out of her mouth in a tempting manner.

It takes everything I have not to want to throw her on the bed and taste the mint on her lips.

I don't. I know she isn't feeling well and that's the last thing on her mind. Instead, I settle in next to her, eating ice cream and watching what is quite possibly the world's dumbest movie.

We've never been like this. Whenever we're together, it's always about sex. And that's been fine the last few years.

All of a sudden, it's not enough. All because of what I feel for this woman. The flashes of time I've gotten with her outside of hotel rooms makes me want more.

I don't want to get an ego boost from someone who is just going to dump me when she finds someone more age appropriate. I want this with her.

I'm discovering there is so much more to this woman than football. I want more glimpses. More time. More than just meeting behind closed doors.

I want more.

# Chapter Nine

## FRANKIE

"**A**lright boys, listen up." I stare around the defensive line as Coach Jenkins calls our linebackers to attention. "Chicago has made some changes to their lineup."

"Yeah, because their quarterback sucks," someone snickers from the back.

"Regardless," he interjects, "Chicago will still be a tough team. I want to make sure we're ready, so Coach Rose is going to be working on some drills with everyone today."

I don't miss the groans.

"Can't you run them, Coach? You're easier on us than Frankie," Newman complains.

"Just for that, you're running extra." My face doesn't change as I yell back to him.

"Ahh, man."

"You should know better by now. Frankie is the one you don't want to mess with," Knox tells him.

"Can I claim I'm a rookie and don't know any better?"

"No," I tell him from where I am standing. "Something you'll eventually learn."

Coach Jenkins blows his whistle and the guys disperse.

The wind blows leaves across the field. Fall is in full swing. Now that we are several weeks into the season, everyone is settling into their roles on the team.

It's been a few weeks. Denver is leading the division and we're in a good position before we start a long few weeks of travel. We leave almost immediately after the Chicago game to head to London. We'll have a few days off, but it's still going to affect our schedules for the week after, even with a bye.

"What are we running today, Coach?" Knox appears at my side. Long sleeves hide his tattoos. A damn shame.

"With Chicago changing up their offensive line, let's work on reaction and footwork drills."

Knox winks at me before pulling on his helmet. "You heard Coach. On the line, boys."

When Knox speaks up, these guys listen. He's been the captain for the last few years. He's earned the respect of this team. I've seen guys in the league longer than him squander away their talent.

But not Knox. He's one of the most talented linebackers I've ever worked with. And we've had some of the best on our team.

Watching as the boys line up, I can't help the smile that spreads across my face. It's always a challenge with new guys on the team. You never know how personalities are going to gel.

It's not a concern with these guys. They run through the drills seamlessly. If someone messes up, the next guy steps up to help.

I only correct if necessary.

"How are things looking over here, Coach Rose?" Coach Brooks pops up next to me.

"Good."

"That's it?"

I smile up at him. "I hate to toot my own horn…"

"Toot away. You've earned it."

"We're looking really good. Chicago doesn't stand a chance against our line."

Coach claps me on the shoulder. "That's what I like to hear, Frankie."

We watch as Newman runs the drill, his footwork improving since he first came to us. He had some bad habits from college that had to be unlearned.

"I'm really impressed. You're bringing these guys along."

"It's what I love to do."

"Keep it up. You're going places."

"Thanks, Coach." I'm not good at taking his praise.

"I mean it. Keep your nose to the grindstone and you'll be a shoo-in for the linebackers coach position."

I swallow down the regret. My eyes search out Knox. He's laughing with the guys on the field. It's a laugh I love hearing.

Until the last few weeks, everything between Knox and me had been strictly sex. It's cleaner that way. It keeps feelings out of it.

After last week? After spending the night eating ice cream, it's starting to get messy. The rules I put into place all those years ago made it so easy.

A fling during football season? Easy. We're just having fun. I know Knox will eventually settle down with someone more appropriate—someone more his age—and I'll, well, I don't know.

When did everything get so damn hard? Because of the man standing next to me.

I have so much respect for Coach Brooks that it makes it that much harder to carry on this fling.

"I love my job, Coach."

"You're more dedicated than a lot of the guys here."

"I don't mean to show them up."

He holds up a hand to stop me. "I'm not saying that. What I'm trying to say is I appreciate your dedication. Keep it up, Frankie."

"Thanks, Coach."

I blow out a breath as he walks over to the offense.

Shit.

Knox's eyes find mine, his brows rising in question.

I shake my head, not wanting to alert him to the thoughts now racing through my head.

Football has been my entire life. Right up until the moment that Knox Fisher walked onto my field. But lately? I've been fighting my growing feelings toward him.

Now, with another rung on the ladder so close, I can see my goal.

Maybe this is why I've always been single. I've never been the one to want a relationship. Football is cut and dried. You run a play and it either works or it doesn't.

Feelings? Feelings aren't so easy—like these big feelings for Knox that are getting harder and harder to deny.

Why can't my feelings for Knox be as easy as a sack against an opposing quarterback?

Why can't I have both Knox and football?

# Chapter Ten

KNOX

**M**y knock is soft in the quiet of the hallway. Curfew was twenty minutes ago. I had to wait and make sure the coast was clear. The door opens and I slide inside.

"Took you long enough." Frankie is on me as soon as I'm in the room, her lips all over mine in a fervent kiss. It's only been a few hours since I last saw her, but it's been too long. There's an urgency to her kiss that I'm not used to feeling.

"You okay?" I pull back.

"I'm fine. Just waiting on you."

"Sorry. Didn't want to get caught."

"If you took any longer, I was going to have to start without you."

Fuck. If her getting off with me that one time was any indication of how it'd be, I'd gladly watch.

Every. Damn. Time.

"Don't tease me," I whisper against her lips.

Frankie pushes me off her. My ass hits the bed. "I do have an idea for tonight."

"Oh yeah?"

She takes two steps closer, standing in between my legs. A mask hangs from her finger. "I'm thinking a game."

"I'm already liking it." I go to grab it from her hand, but she pulls back.

"How about you wear it?"

"You serious?" I grab her hips and drop my head between her tits.

"You like games. So I thought we'd play one tonight."

"Yes." My answer rushes out of me. Sex games with Frankie?

No question—I want to play.

"Good. Now strip."

Holding her still, I stand. "Always so bossy."

Frankie quirks a brow at me. "What can I say? I like bossing you around."

Stripping out of my shirt and pants, I drop down into the center of the bed, a cushion of pillows behind me. My cock is already hard in my boxers.

"Safe word is Chicago."

"Really?"

"Gotta have one." She sits on the bed next to me.

"Why the team we're playing tomorrow?" I cross my arms behind my head.

She smiles. "Easy to remember."

"So what's the game?"

Frankie runs a hand up my chest, tracing my nipple. "You have to guess what I'm rubbing over your chest."

"And what do I get if I guess right?"

Frankie hovers over me, hooking the mask behind my head. "I'm sure you can figure that out. Here's a little hint."

Her free hand dips, rubbing over the bulge in my boxers.

"Fuck."

"Good. Now, close your eyes."

Obeying her command, she slips the mask over my eyes. Everything goes dark. Even if I could open my eyes, I wouldn't want to.

"Can't see anything?"

"No."

"Good. I'll give you an easy one to start."

There's a rustling next to me that I turn toward before something wet and cold tracks down my chest.

"Shit. Did it have to be ice?"

"Just giving you an idea of what to expect."

The next thing I know, my boxers are being pulled off, and Frankie sucks one of my balls into her warm mouth.

"Fuck, that feels good."

All too soon, she pops off.

"That's it?"

"Patience, Knox. Patience." She squeezes my balls before pulling her hand away.

"If I die of blue balls…"

"You'll what?" she asks. I tilt my head toward her voice, only imagining the look on her face.

"I'll haunt you."

"What a threat," she says as she laughs.

The bed dips again as Frankie's body leans into mine. Even with no sight, I know those curves. The delicious feel of them.

"What's this?"

She rolls something down my chest. This time it's not as easy.

"How many guesses do I get?"

"Already giving up?" Her breath is hot on my ear.

"Hell no. Just need to know how many tries I get."

She rolls it again. "Two. After that we move on."

"A coin?"

"Are you sure?" Her tongue licks across the shell of my ear.

"Yes." Even though I'm not close to sure at all.

"Correct."

"Fuck yes!" I pump my arm in victory as Frankie grabs my chin. Her lips are on me, her tongue licking across the seam of my mouth. I open to her. She takes control and I let her have it. While she explores my mouth like she's never tasted it, I fight the need to take over. One kiss and I know my dick is leaking all over my stomach.

I sink into the kiss with each swipe of her tongue. Fuck, do I ever love kissing this woman. I could do it forever and still not get sick of it.

"Very good, Knox."

The way she says my name has heat rushing through me. I want more. Every part of me is aching to have more of her.

"Alright, how about this?"

Frankie's legs settle on either side of my chest as she drags herself over me.

I'd know that anywhere.

"Your pussy."

"That was fast."

"I have a bit of an obsession with it."

"Since you answered so quickly, I'll let you pick your reward."

"Your pussy."

I can sense her eye roll. "You already answered."

"I want your pussy as my reward. I want you to sit on my face while I make you come."

"I don't think you understand how this game works."

"I get a prize for guessing correctly. I guessed your pussy and now I want it. Move it, Frankie."

I blindly reach out, finding her legs, and pull her up

and over my chest. The sweet scent of her fills my nose more than usual.

We should really play this game more often. With this as a reward? I'm all in.

I drag my nose through her folds, my hands moving to her ass.

"I love your pussy."

"You've mentioned that."

Taking my time, I pull her closer. My tongue dips inside her as she releases a gasp.

"You like that?" I whisper against her.

"God, yes."

She's already dripping as I suck her clit into my mouth, swirling my tongue around it. I pull her closer.

I run my tongue lower, my assault on her pussy slow and luxurious. I take my time, licking and sucking.

I know it's driving her wild because she sits down farther on my face.

"Why are you so good at this?" she whispers.

I don't answer, just continue driving her closer to an orgasm. I know this game was meant for me, but I want her to get off. Even if my dick is aching for his own release.

"Knox. Oh God." She's a whimpering mess as I drive my tongue inside her again, tasting her. "Oh God."

She comes on my tongue. I hold her hips, not letting her move as I soak up every last drop of her orgasm. Her body goes lax over me.

"Holy shit." Frankie slides down my body, the mask now askew over my eyes. It's too hard to make her out.

"I'm really liking this game, Frankie."

"What do you want next?" she asks, breathless.

"What do you want?"

Her fingers trail up my chest, pulling the mask off. "I want you inside me."

I flip us over, and now I can her. She already looks thoroughly fucked, and we haven't even gotten to the best part.

"Again, how is this a game?" Lifting one of her legs to my shoulder, I thrust inside her.

"A game where we're both winners?"

"Fuck, I'll take it."

We're already living on borrowed time, so I don't waste any more of it. My hips piston into her. Each squeeze of that perfect pussy of hers is pulling me closer and closer to release.

Dropping my forehead to hers, I watch as I slide in and out of her. What a fucking sight.

"Harder."

I pick up the pace, moving in closer.

Frankie's whispered words—*harder, right there, yes*—have me close to the edge. But I'm not going over without her.

"C'mon," I growl out. I suck on the soft skin of her tit, nibbling on it.

"Gah!" Her nails dig harder into my back.

"That's it, Frankie. That's it." I swivel my hips with each thrust.

Brown eyes stay locked on mine. The tension swirls around us. Lust. Heat. Desire. It's all there. Not to mention something else that lingers just under the surface.

Before I can grab onto it, she's coming. Her quiet shouts are lost on me, my own orgasm roaring through me.

"Fuck. Fuck, fuck, fuck," I shout.

Holy shit. I'm coming harder than I ever have before.

"Oh God, Knox." Frankie's pussy squeezes me twice more, before I pull out of her and collapse next to her.

I'm completely spent. Every last drop of my energy was given to the woman now lying next to me.

Frankie tilts her head, soft eyes looking at me.

"That was…" Frankie starts.

"I know."

It's hard to put into words. What we just did feels like more than just sex. There was trust there, yes, but something more.

A deepening of this connection between the two of us. I pull her into my arms, needing her right now. It almost feels like the two of us can have more.

Fuck the age difference.

Fuck the fact that she's my coach and we shouldn't be doing it.

Fuck every other reason I tell myself this won't work.

All I want is the woman in my arms.

"Shouldn't you be getting back to your room?" She's breathless. While her words are pushing me out, her arm wraps around mine, holding me to her.

"In a few minutes," I whisper.

Frankie spins in my arms, resting her head on my chest. I can feel the happy smile on her lips.

"Whatcha thinking?" I ask.

I feel her smile against my chest. "Best game ever."

# Chapter Eleven

## KNOX

"Alright, boys. Today is going to be a hard game."

That's an understatement. What started as an icy rain has turned into snow. It's caked on the field and made pregame warm-ups that much harder. Forget an actual game.

"Chicago plays in this weather, just like we do. Nothing will be given. Everything will be earned."

Coach looks around at each and every one of us.

"Play your game today. You've got what it takes."

Alex steps into the center of the room, standing over the Mountain Lion emblem.

"You heard what Coach said. It'll be a tough game. But help the man next to you and we've got what it takes to bring home the win. Mountain Lions on three…"

He counts down and "Mountain Lions" echoes around the locker room. We file out toward the field. The wind turns bitter as we charge out of the tunnel as one team.

The snow is coming down hard and fast, covering the field as quickly as they can clear it. Overhead lights cut through the late afternoon darkness. Fans are a blur in the stands.

It's like Denver completely skipped fall and went right to winter.

But their cheers can be heard through the stadium. They're vibrating with excitement for the game today.

Alex and Jackson head out to midfield for the coin toss. The coin gets lost in the snow, but I see the refs point to Chicago.

Perfect.

Alex and Jackson run back to the sideline.

"Think you can keep them on the sideline?" he chides.

I give him a smile. "It's what I'm known for. Maybe then you can figure out how to play quarterback."

"Asshole."

"Doing what I can, Captain."

"Head in the game, boys." Frankie comes by, eyeing all of us. "Good strong start to get the momentum in our direction."

"You got it, boss."

I hold back on the wink, but her gaze lingers on me a moment longer.

Probably because of all the things I did to her last night.

Fuck. Not something I need to be thinking about ten seconds before running onto the field.

Chicago is stopped at the twelve, their returner slipping and falling before he can hit open field.

Grabbing my helmet, I run out into the field. Watching their offense set up, I call out to my guys.

"Looks like they're going to pass. Watch the short route."

The ball is snapped and, as predicted, Chicago goes with a quick route to start the game.

We don't let them have any. The second the ball lands in the hands of the receiver, I'm there.

Loss of one yard.

The crowd goes nuts as we force a three and out on the first series of the game.

"Great job, boys." Frankie walks over to where we're sitting on the bench. "I think they're going to scrap that play because they got nowhere with it. We'll need to watch for the run."

Frankie turns her deep brown eyes on me.

"Think you can manage that?"

"Hell yeah. Nothing to worry about, Coach."

"Great. Then get it done."

Frankie moves down the sideline as Newman knocks me in the shoulder. "Damn. Even with that stop, you get no love."

If only he knew.

"Only makes me want to work harder."

We watch the offense take the field, and Alex operates as if this weather is nothing but another Sunday for him.

He's precise and exacting as he marches the offense down the field.

Right into the end zone. The stands explode in cheers as Logan makes the touchdown look easy.

"Hell yeah, kid!" I smack him on the helmet as he runs back to the sideline, a smile stretching across his face.

"Felt damn good." He unclasps his chinstrap and drops down on the bench beside me.

"Great move on the linebacker," I praise his move.

"Just like you taught me."

This is why I love being captain. Even though Logan is on the offense, it's easy to show him moves to help him. The kid is like a sponge…absorbing everything everyone tells him.

This time, when we kick off, Chicago takes a knee in the end zone.

Frankie's intuition was right. Instead of a pass, Chicago goes for the run.

Anticipating this, I go to make the block, but I slip on the snow. The running back breaks away as he takes off down the sideline. Our safety finally gets him, shoving him out of bounds right into our sideline.

Chaos breaks out as I jog to the sideline. Refs are there, pulling players away from Chicago's guy.

In the center of it all, Frankie is lying on the ground. Someone is calling the team doctor over to her as she tries to wave them off.

My heart jumps into my throat. I want to rush over too. Check her out to see if she's okay with my own eyes.

"I'm fine." She fights the wince. I know she doesn't want to be seen as weak among the guys.

"What the hell happened?" I push players out of the way.

Frankie glares at me, telling me my presence is not wanted.

"Fisher, get back on the field. We'll take care of Coach Rose."

The team doctor shoves me out of the way, asking questions. "Did she lose consciousness?"

"She's right here, and can answer for herself," Frankie grumbles.

"Her head snapped back and hit the turf." A coach ignores her, answering the doctor's question.

"I'm fine," she reiterates to the doctor.

"I'd feel better if I looked you over." The doctor's words are more forceful this time.

"Knox! Field!" Jenkins yells at me.

I'm pushed out onto the field as Frankie is helped to her feet.

The next snaps go by in a blur. Chicago leaves the field without a score as I run back to our sideline. I don't know if I followed the called plays or not.

My mind was on one thing and one thing only.

I've seen the hits people take on the sideline. It's part of the game, but it doesn't make it any easier.

Our defensive coordinator greets us.

"Coach Rose will be out for the rest of the game."

"How's she doing?" Newman asks the question I can't.

"Doctors are with her now."

He doesn't give us anything further. The game goes by in a swirl of snow and wind.

The Mountain Lions pull off a win, no thanks to me.

My hands feel like they're in blocks of ice as I strip out of my jersey and head for the showers.

I let the hot water wash over me, soothing every cold and tired muscle.

I usually love playing in this weather. Something about the elements make it feel like I'm back on the peewee field —reminding me why I love this game.

Not today.

Today, the game couldn't end fast enough.

Because for once, football isn't the most important thing.

Frankie is.

Grabbing my towel, I wrap it around my waist and head back toward my locker.

"You okay, Knox?" Alex slaps me on the chest. "You seem out of it."

"I think my brain iced over. I don't know if I'll ever warm up." I laugh off Alex's comment.

"You sure?"

I don't like his questioning look. Alex is too insightful for his own good. "Positive. Go home to your man."

That puts a huge grin on his face. And puts me in the clear.

"You're not going to hear me argue with that."

"Tell Carter I said hi."

"I will." Alex puts on his coat and takes off.

The locker room empties out after post-game interviews are completed. There's still no sign of Frankie. Pulling my sweats on, I make up my mind.

Fuck.

I know the rules.

*Her rules.*

We limit our time together as much as possible. Makes it easier to cover our tracks.

Fuck that.

Pulling a sweatshirt over my head, I grab my keys and head out.

Rules be damned.

## Chapter Twelve

### FRANKIE

If this is what being a football player is like, I never want to suit up.

Except if I were a player, I would have been wearing pads when I took that hit.

I don't blame the kid from Chicago. These things happen. It's all part of the game.

But my entire body hurts. Thank God I didn't have a concussion. I was given strict instructions to rest and come in for the trip to London this week.

I can handle that.

The fireplace crackles inside my tiny bungalow. I sink farther into the oversized chair as the snow falls outside. I could easily fall asleep here with the muscle relaxer the doctor gave me.

Except for the knock on the door that disrupts my peace.

Groaning, I push myself out of the chair and shuffle to the door.

I can't hide my shock at seeing Knox—hood up and snow stuck to his shoulders— at my door.

"What are you doing here?"

"Mind if I come in? It's cold as fuck out here."

"Sure." I step aside and Knox marches into my house like he owns the place.

"Are you okay?" Knox shoves his hood back and fixes dark brown eyes on me. Normally, they'd be stirring something low in my belly, but not tonight.

Tonight, they almost appear angry.

"I'm fine, Knox."

"You're not fine, Frankie. I've taken hits like that." I can see his jaw grinding, his annoyance palpable. "Tell me. Really."

I bite down on my lip, trying to hold in my emotions.

"A bit sore." I don't miss the shake in my voice. And based on Knox's face, he doesn't believe me either.

"Bullshit."

"Knox…" Whatever fight I have is drained out.

Knox steps closer to me. His brown eyes are fixed on mine. A cold hand sweeps the hair back from my neck. "You don't always have to be strong, Frankie."

"Yes I do." My voice cracks.

Wrapping an arm around my waist, Knox pulls me close. "Let me be strong for you," he whispers.

I break. All the emotions I've been trying to keep in check all day come pouring out of my eyes.

"It's okay." With Knox's arms around me, I feel safe.

I fist my hands in his sweatshirt, trying to absorb all of his heat. "How do you take hits like that?"

"I have a lot more padding than you do," he mutters into my hair. "But I have a way to make you feel better."

"Oh, yeah?" My laugh is watery.

"C'mon." Knox pulls back, taking my hand in his. My eyes stay on his as he leads me past the kitchen and into my bedroom. Bypassing the bed, he leads me into my bathroom. He was here once before years ago, and he clearly hasn't forgotten where he's going.

"A good soak will help you feel better."

Knox turns the water on in the oversized tub, adding a touch of cold water to the hot.

"Is this what makes you feel better?"

Knox smirks at me, pulling his sweatshirt over his head. "I usually take an ice bath, but I don't think you'd want that."

"Not particularly, no."

Grabbing one of the bath bombs sitting in the bowl next to the tub, he dumps it in. Lavender fumes explode in the room. Knox strips down to his boxers and turns back to me.

"Baths are kind of hard if you're fully clothed."

I pull the oversized T-shirt I'm wearing over my head and drop it to the floor. I take a step closer to Knox, pulling my leggings and underwear down.

My legs wobble and Knox catches me before I fall. "I've got you."

His arms tighten around my waist as he hauls me into the tub with him. Knox settles in and pulls me down—gently—between his legs.

"Oh God." The moment the warm water envelops my body, it seems every muscle starts to relax.

"Feel better?" I don't miss the gravel in his tone.

"Much." I breathe a sigh of relief.

"That was a hard fucking hit, Frankie."

"It's part of the game."

"It's part of my game." Knox's hand drifts around my stomach, pulling me closer to him before he shuts the water off. It laps gently against my chest. "I could barely concentrate during the game. They showed the highlight, and it wasn't a soft hit."

"You should have been focusing on the game."

"We won. Sorry, but I was more concerned about you."

"How do you think it feels watching you take those hits every week?"

Knox scoffs. "I have pads on. I know what I'm doing. You're not that worried."

I shift, resting more comfortably against him. "You're right. I'm not. Because I know it's all a part of the game."

"I think this is an agree to disagree situation, Francesca."

"Ooh. Full named me. I guess you mean business."

"What am I going to do with you?"

"Please don't tackle me." I laugh.

"I promise I would never tackle you."

I drop my head back onto Knox's muscular shoulder, sinking into his touch. For the first time all afternoon, I relax. It was all pokes and prods at the stadium to make sure nothing was broken. I can't imagine being a player having to go through the entire regular season, never mind if you make the playoffs.

"I'll be okay." I wrap a hand over Knox's, holding him to me. "I promise. If the doctors didn't think I'd be okay, they wouldn't have sent me home."

Knox blows out a breath. "I know. It's just hard to see someone you lo—care about get hurt," he cuts himself off.

His words are fuzzy in my head, the warm water and scent of lavender starting to take over my senses. Coupled with the muscle relaxer, I could fall asleep here. Safely in Knox's arms.

It's just the two of us. No football. No outside noise. No people telling us we can't be together.

Just us.

Knox and Frankie.

For the first time, it shuts down all the thoughts that keep cropping up. I don't care about how much older I am —that Knox was a sophomore in high school when I got my first coaching job. I don't care that I've never been a relationship person because my focus has always been football.

None of that matters as I sit here in Knox's arms.

"Can I do anything else to help?" Knox sweeps my hair over my shoulder, dropping a kiss on my neck.

"You're doing it right now."

Every time we're together, the reasons why we *shouldn't* be together are always there. But right now, I can't bring myself to care.

Because I'm exactly where I want to be.

Wrapped up, warm and safe, in Knox's arms.

# Chapter Thirteen

## KNOX

"How come we've never gotten to travel with you before?" Grandma complains next to me.

"You've never wanted to come with me before."

"Who wants to go to Vegas? I've been there. Now London…"

She takes in the palace in front of her.

"What she means to say is…we're happy Denver was playing in London and that we were able to come along for the ride," Mom interjects.

With the Mountain Lions getting one of the few games played in London this year, the team decided to come early so we'd have the chance to sightsee a few days. Considering the farthest I've ever been outside the country is Canada, it's a nice change of pace.

Plus, I was able to bring Mom and Grandma. I don't get a lot of time with them during the season, so I'm happy with these few extra days.

"That too." Grandma squints, looking closer at the palace. "Do you think we'll see the pink-haired princess?"

"She's not a princess anymore," Mom states.

"Maybe I should dye my hair pink." Grandma turns and we start our trek down the Mall.

"I don't think you'd look good with pink hair."

I'm glad Mom said it and not me. The two of them couldn't look more different. While I look like my grandparents, my mom stands out with blonde hair and blue eyes.

"I'd look positively delightful with pink hair."

"You wouldn't be missed in a crowd."

"Maybe it'll distract everyone and I can win in bingo."

I fight the laugh. "You'll resort to cheating then to win?"

"Not cheating if I have the skills to back it up. Now, give me your arm. I'm eighty-seven and need help on these old streets."

"You're not tired? We can always go back to the hotel."

She scoffs. "Nothing a quick bite to eat won't help."

I continue on the path toward the Thames. It's crowded with people since we're in the central part of the city. It's a perfect day to be out and exploring. No sun, but warm enough that you're not cold. Better than Denver these last few days. Hopefully the winter weather will clear up by the time we're home and we can actually enjoy fall.

Sprinkled throughout the crowds is a mish-mash of football jerseys. No one team stands out, but I've seen a few Alex Young jerseys among them.

We pass over the river and head toward the Eye. It's only slightly less crowded on this side of the river.

"It's a shame no one has recognized you." Grandma squeezes my arm. "I thought you'd be more popular here."

"Are you trying to tell me no one likes me?" I ask my grandma.

"Oh hush." She swats at me. "I was only thinking I could find a nice British girl for you to marry."

"Are you trying to marry Knox off?" Frankie appears in front of us. Pink stains her cheeks. Her hair is pulled back in a messy contraption on the top of her head. An oversized sweater hides her curves, but she looks sexy as hell.

"Frankie! What a pleasant surprise running into you!" Grandma drops my arm and wraps her in a hug.

"It's nice to see you again." Her eyes shift to mine before looking toward my mom. "Hi, I'm Knox's coach, Frankie."

She extends her hand out.

"Shannon. It's nice to meet you. I'm glad you have more manners than my son."

I roll my eyes. "Maybe if you'd given me more than two seconds, I would have introduced you."

"We've heard a lot about you." Mom ignores me.

Frankie turns wide eyes on me. "I hope not all bad."

"Not—"

"He says you're the best coach he's ever had," Mom interrupts me.

The pink on her cheeks deepens. "Now I know you're lying."

"Not a lie if it's the truth." My tone is firm.

Frankie is one of the best coaches I've ever had. Even more so than the actual linebackers coach. Sure, he's good, but Frankie knows the game of football better than anyone. I know she works harder to prove herself because she's a woman in a man's field, but she could run circles around any coach out there.

"We were just going to get some tea. Would you like to join us?" Mom asks.

"We were?"

She side-eyes me. "Yes. It's a British thing to do, and we're in London." She states this like I'm an idiot.

"I wouldn't want to impose."

Grandma waves her off before linking their arms together. "Nonsense. We'd love to have you. Maybe we can get Knox to talk about something other than football."

"You two are the ones that have brought up football more than me today."

"Oh hush," Grandma chides. "Now, you'll join us. I need to get off my feet."

"That sounds wonderful. I could use some tea after being out in the cold all day." Frankie gives her a warm smile that does funny things to my insides.

I follow behind the two of them, Mom at my side. "Something making you happy?"

"Who says I'm happy?"

"I know you. You're fighting a smile. You didn't have that when it was just the three of us."

"I don't know what you're talking about."

Except I know exactly what she's talking about. Grandma is chatting Frankie's ear off. Whatever they're talking about has Frankie throwing her head back in laughter. I like seeing the two of them together.

My mom and my grandma are the two most important people in my life. Aside from the guys, I keep my circle small. You never know who wants a piece of you because of your status in life.

Frankie is one of the few people I've let in. She knows what the demands of this job are because she lives it every day.

"Frankie, are you seeing anyone?" Grandma asks as we enter the tea shop.

"Grandma! You can't ask her that." I swear, I can't take this woman anywhere.

"What?" She shrugs her shoulders. "I'm just making conversation."

"It's okay, Knox." Frankie gives me a cunning look. Fuck, this woman is going to be the death of me. "I'm not seeing anyone, Darlene. You know anyone?"

Grandma claps her hands as a hostess greets us and leads us to a small table in the back. Growling, I follow them.

"Careful, Knox, your teeth are showing."

My gaze snaps back to my mom. She has a knowing look on her face.

Damn these women in my life. They can read me like an open book.

"Knox, why are you not more agreeable?" I pull out the chair for my grandma when we get to the table—like the gentleman she raised me to be—but she shoos me away. "Help Frankie there. I can manage."

Taking a deep breath, I go to help the woman in question with her chair. "May I?"

This close, I can see the flecks of gold in her eyes. Fuck, she really is the most beautiful woman ever. "You may." She winks at me.

After helping her into her chair, I take my own seat. I ignore the two sets of eyes I feel on me. I don't want to see the looks my mom and grandma are giving me. I take the coward's way out and stare at the menu handed to me while they make small talk.

There's no question that if we were at home right now, there's no way I'd be seen with Frankie like this. In Denver, I'm recognized most places I go. In London, people aren't as into American football. They love their own *football.*

Here, it's the four of us tucked away in a tiny tea shop without a care in the world.

The waiter comes by and takes our order.

"How long have you been coaching?" Grandma asks Frankie.

"I'm in my thirteenth year now."

"Thirteen? There's no way you're that old."

"I'm thirty-five."

Grandma looks at me before looking back at Frankie. "Why does Knox look older than you?"

Frankie tries to cover her laugh but can't.

"Really, Grandma?"

"What? Women age better. It's a fact."

"I appreciate that." Frankie's response is much more diplomatic than mine.

"We also get smarter as we age too."

"Pretty sure men do too," I mumble.

"Mom, give Knox a break. You don't want to embarrass him in front of his coach."

"I think we've crossed that bridge, Mom," I mutter.

"I guess it's something you learn with age then." Frankie smiles at me. "You can never stop your family from embarrassing you."

I always forget about the age difference between us, but she seems to like to remind me.

Frankie is one of the few people I keep close. From the beginning, she was always there to talk to, and she understands what players go through. It's what makes her such a good coach. Even when we weren't hooking up, I would always go to her for advice.

I trust her. Implicitly.

Two pots of tea are dropped off. "Please let me know if you need anything else."

"Thank you." I smile at him as he walks off.

Mom pours tea into each of the four cups and holds her cup out for a toast.

"Well, what a wonderful day this turned out to be. We're so happy you could join us, Frankie. And here's to a win for the Mountain Lions. Cheers."

We all clink cups as Frankie looks to me. We share a secret smile before sipping our tea.

Spending the afternoon with my mom, my grandma, and Frankie in London?

Wonderful day indeed.

# Chapter Fourteen

### KNOX

"You know, you don't have to hang out with us all night," Mom says as the black taxi pulls up to the curb.

"Are you trying to ditch me?" I laugh.

"Would you be mad if we said yes?" Grandma pats me on the cheek. "We want to go out and hit the clubs."

I can hear Frankie laughing behind me.

"I would hate to dampen your evening. I don't think the clubs are ready for you two." I shift my focus to my mom. "I assume you'll be in charge?"

"I promise we'll both make it back to the hotel in one piece." Mom gives me Scout's honor. "Nice to meet you, Frankie."

"You too, Shannon," she calls back.

I give them each a kiss on the cheek. "I'll see you in the morning."

"Love you. Have fun and don't get into too much trouble." They wave and shut the door behind them. Stuffing my hands in my pockets, I spin on my heel and turn back to Frankie.

She's glowing in the street lights. "Care to take a car back to the hotel with me?"

Frankie looks around. "It's a nice night. Want to walk?"

Hell, I'd swim through the Thames if it meant I got to spend more time with her. I nod.

"Enjoying your time in London so far?" Frankie's voice is quiet as we head out along the water.

There's a bite to the air now that the sun has set.

"I think my mom and grandma are having more fun than I am."

"It's nice you were able to bring them."

"They gave up a lot for me, so I'm glad I can do something nice for them."

"I'm sure they don't see it that way. They love you."

"Even if they cause me headaches," I admit with a laugh.

Frankie points behind her. "You mean you didn't want to go to the clubs with them?"

I groan, turning and walking backward. "I don't even want to think about that."

"Do you really think they went?"

I nod. "I have no doubt."

"You can't tell me you're not having fun though."

I stop in front of Big Ben. "I've never been here, so yeah. It's pretty cool we get to play here."

Frankie stands shoulder to shoulder with me. "A lot of teams hate coming here."

"Really?"

"Oh yeah. Most teams come in on Friday, play, then fly home. It's a lot of travel for one game."

"It's a bonus we actually get to spend time here. And then we get our bye week after. I think it's a pretty good deal."

"Don't forget about the gala next week that we all have to go to."

I groan. "Fuck. I keep forgetting about that. I know it's for a good cause, but I hate wearing a monkey suit."

Frankie eyes me up and down. "Considering how good you look in your game day suit, I think you'll look pretty good."

"Do you have a date for it?" I bite out.

This is part of the reason why I've been blocking it out. All of the guys are going with their partners. I have no one to go with. Not when I can't go with the one person I want to.

I want to take the woman standing next to me. I want to pick her up, like a real date, and be able to show her off to everyone.

To add insult to injury, she'll be there all night. Just out of my reach.

But we can't.

"Do you?"

Glancing around me, the sidewalk is empty. Well, mostly empty.

I close the distance between us, tucking a piece of hair that escaped behind her ear. I drag my fingers down her neck. "Answer my question first."

Frankie's eyes widen as her tongue sneaks out to wet those soft lips.

"No."

"Good."

"I take it you don't either?" She tilts her head up.

"No. Not when I want to go with you."

"Knox…" I don't miss the exasperation in her voice.

"It's true. I know we can't go together, but it doesn't mean I don't want to."

Frankie hesitates, holding a hand over my chest before

drawing it back. I hate that it has to be this way. That we can't be together like everyone else I know.

Instead of focusing on it, I see something. An oasis for just the two of us.

"C'mon."

"Where are we going?"

"Trust me?"

She nods as we close the short distance to the attraction looming large over the river.

"The Eye?"

I smile as I walk up the empty walkway.

"Just two?" the man at the front of the line asks.

"Is it possible to get a private…bubble?" I have no idea what the glass things are called.

"Pod. Gonna cost ya, mate." His accent is thick.

"Got it." I pull out my wallet and hand over my credit card.

He smiles at me and charges the card. "They'll help you over there."

A few people are getting off as we're waved into the next pod.

"This is your solution to not being able to go to the gala together?" Frankie walks to the glass as the door closes behind us. "Being together under the cover of darkness?"

"It's not like I plan on robbing banks." The pod starts to move. The city fades away as we start our rise over the river. I stalk over to her, dropping my hands on the railing on either side of her. "I want to spend time with you."

This time, when Frankie moves, she doesn't hesitate. Her hands land on my chest. It hasn't been that long since we've been together, but I miss her.

With the start of every new season, I get deeper and deeper into this thing. I always wonder what would've happened if we hadn't been stranded in Buffalo a few years ago. If we'd be here now.

Frankie is too good for me. Too beautiful. You name it. I'm so far out of my league with her, it's not even funny.

I keep waiting for the day when Frankie realizes this. Thank God she hasn't yet.

"I'm glad I bumped into you today." She tips her head up. I fucking love that she's almost as tall as I am.

The air is charged between us as we continue circling.

"I'm glad you did too."

My mouth is an inch from hers, breathing her in. Her hands tighten in my shirt.

"Knox."

I take that as permission and take her in a searing kiss. I don't care that we're not paying attention to the sights around us.

The only thing I care about is her.

Fuck.

She tastes sweet like tea as my tongue finds hers. Each swipe, each touch has me getting hard. Which is inconvenient because there isn't much we can do about it right now.

I move my hands into her hair. The kiss becomes more urgent as we start to sink back down to earth. I'm not ready to let her go yet. I want to stay here with her, with her lips on mine, and never move.

But all too soon, we're breaking apart. Frankie's lips are swollen and wet. I want to take her back to my hotel room and have my way with her. I can't. Not with an early morning practice tomorrow.

I step back, trying to cool the fire now sweeping through me. Frankie is still staring at me with that same fire.

We come to a stop. The doors open.

The man from earlier is there to greet us. "Enjoyed the sights?"

I'm grinning as we step out of the pod.

"Most beautiful sight in the world."

And I didn't see a goddamn thing.

# Chapter Fifteen

KNOX

"When you said sightseeing, I didn't think you meant this."

Union Jack flags hang over the street, intermixed with the Mountain Lions flag and Miami's. The street is bursting with people. Jerseys from both teams are represented.

"We never get to do anything cool like this." Colin looks around, his eyes wide in awe. "I've never left the country. Why not see the NFL Street in London?"

"Because there are about a million other things to see in London?" Jackson tells him. Colin grabbed Logan, Alex, Jackson, and me from the hotel, claiming he wanted to go sightseeing.

Not that it would bother me not seeing anything else. I did my sightseeing yesterday with my mom and grandma and then sneaking off with Frankie. If I don't see another thing, I'll be happy.

"Bollocks. Peyton and I did everything we wanted to do yesterday. Besides, she's working with the league on game stuff."

Alex shakes his head as we squeeze through the crowd of people. A few people have stopped us, but not many. "Two days in London and you're ready to move here."

"Waffles would love London."

"You realize the league doesn't have a team in London, right?" Alex asks him.

Colin thinks about it. "Maybe I could start my own team after I retire."

I snort laugh. "Good luck. There's no way you have enough money to start your own team."

"Maybe I'll just become a general manager and move my team here."

He goes off into his own little world.

"You didn't want to bring Carter?" I ask Alex as we head deeper into the crowds.

A sad look washes over his face. "I wish, but it didn't line up with his work schedule and he couldn't get off."

"That fucking sucks."

"You're telling me. I told him we can come back here in the summer."

"Must be nice to have summers off."

Alex gives me the side-eye. "We do have an off season."

I give him the side-eye right back. "And maybe a handful of those weeks we actually get off. Don't tell me you're not still training every day we're off."

"Okay, yes, but I don't want to not be ready for when the season starts."

I can only laugh at him. Alex is the epitome of dedicated football player. So much so that he hid his true self for years. I don't know if I would have had the same dedication to the game as he does.

"You guys. Look." Colin points ahead of us.

Cutting through the middle of the road, a skills competition is set up. Kids are throwing into targets. Adults are trying to kick a football through a smaller than normal field goal.

And Colin is grinning like a fucking kid at Christmas.

"Oh, please no," I grumble.

"Colin, that's for fans," Alex tells him matter-of-factly. "Not for you."

"Oh, come on! Wouldn't it be fun to see who's the best out of all of us?" He throws his arms out and starts walking backward toward the entrance.

"I'm game. I'll kick all of your asses." Logan throws his hand in the air.

"Please don't encourage him," Alex pleads.

"You realize it's not set up for all of our positions," I point out. "I don't see tackling dummies."

"Because it's not hard to tackle, dummy." Colin slaps me on the shoulder.

"And yet, I don't think you would be able to throw down with a guard when it comes to it."

"I can school all of you guys when it comes to kicking a field goal." Jackson blows on his fingers and brushes them on his shoulder.

Colin points at him. "That I don't doubt."

Jackson gives us a bemused smile. "Therefore I don't feel the need to get involved in whatever this is." He waves a hand around us. "I will, however, be the judge."

"Perfect." Colin rubs his hands together. "Now, let's go, Knoxy. I'm ready to show off my catching skills. I might school you."

"No shit, Sherlock. Of course you're going to do better in the receiving challenge because you're a *wide receiver*." A small crowd has started to gather around us.

"Okay, fine." Colin looks around, finding a kid in an Alex Young jersey. "Hey. You think you can catch?"

The kid looks shell-shocked. "Me?"

"What do you say? Think you can beat Knox here?" Colin elbows me in the side.

He nods his head vigorously. "Yes."

Colin tilts his head from side to side, cracking his neck. "You're going down, Fisher."

"That kid is probably more mature than the two of you combined." Alex rolls his eyes at us.

"I can beat him!" the kid pipes up.

"Alex, think you can throw to him while I throw to Knox?"

"Wait." I stop Colin from going onto the mini field with a hand to his chest. "You're going to screw up so I lose."

"I would do no such thing." Colin is grinning like a maniac.

"No way." I shake my head. "Logan, you're passing to me."

"You sure you want to take that bet, Fisher?" Colin quirks a brow at me.

"You guys didn't actually make a bet," Jackson points out.

"Excellent point, Fields." I cross my arms and turn to Colin. "What'll it be, James?"

He taps his finger on his chin, thinking of something.

"Guys, please remember we are not the only people out here." Alex looks around. A few people in Mountain Lions jerseys are now standing near us with phones out. "Nothing stupid, okay?"

"Loser has to buy a round at the pub. Does that work for you, Dad?" Colin turns his attention back to Alex.

He's grinning like an idiot. I know he's excited about becoming a dad. "I approve."

"I'm guessing Colin will be buying then." I duck under the barrier onto the small field.

The kid waiting for us is beaming. "Hi, Mr. Fisher. I'm Joey."

"Hey Joey. You can call me Knox. Is Alex your favorite player?"

He looks down at the jersey he's wearing. "This is my older brother's. You're my favorite."

I hold my hand out for a high five. He jumps up to meet it. Ruffling his brown hair, I line up across from him and Logan. "You've got good taste. You think you're gonna beat me?"

He nods again. "I'm a receiver and running back in my flag football team at home."

"Damn. Alex has his work cut out for him."

Alex winds up his arm. "He's going to make you look like a chump."

"Oooh! Alex with the trash talk," Colin bellows from the side. "Let's do this, boys."

"Throw me a good one, Logan." I point at him as I step to the line. "Good luck, kid."

We both take off running as Logan and Alex launch their throws down the field. Joey catches Alex's pass with ease as I have to lay it out, only to have Logan's wobbly ball whiff through my fingers.

"I beat you!" Joey is cheering as Alex comes down to congratulate him. "Yes!" He pumps his fist in the air.

"You could be the next Colin James."

He's beaming. "Will you sign the football for me?"

"Sure thing."

Someone from the sideline tosses a marker and we all scrawl our signatures across the ball.

"This is so cool! Thank you." Joey runs over to show it to what I'm only assuming is his family.

"You know what this means, Knox?" Colin walks onto the field.

"I know, I know. I'll be buying drinks tonight."

Colin wraps an arm around my shoulders. "Oh, that was a given. I've seen you try and catch before and you're terrible."

I turn a hard stare to him. "Then what are you getting at?"

"Thank God you don't play offense, because otherwise we'd be last in the league."

"Thank fuck for that."

# Chapter Sixteen

KNOX

"Fuck. It's freezing out here," Logan whines behind me.

"You know we play in Denver, right?" I ask as I stretch my cold muscles. My breath puffs out in front of me.

"It was supposed to be warmer."

I smile. It's a cloudy, cold day. The kind of day that I love playing in. Wembley is packed with fans today. It's going to be a high energy game, no doubt.

"You want to go sit inside by the fire? Maybe have a cup of tea?" I stick out my bottom lip in Logan's direction, mocking him.

"Fuck you, Knox." He laughs, shoving me playfully.

"We're playing Miami today. They probably don't know what this cold weather is like."

"It's going to be a good game today." Logan stretches one arm above his head.

"You ready?"

Logan is finally getting to start a game. He's been in this league long enough, and it's hard when you're playing backup to one of the league's best running backs.

I know the feeling. I took the backseat to Roberts for my first few years, stepping in on third downs and anytime he needed to be out for an injury.

"Beyond fucking ready." He starts doing high knees. "But I also feel like I could puke. That's normal, right?"

"Pretty sure I puked right before I went onto the field. Not the best look, but hey, we won."

"I want to win this one more than any other game."

I nod at him. "I know. Just play your game. That's all you can do."

"Have you always been this zen?"

Sitting down on the field, I start stretching my quads.

"Comes with age, I guess." I wink at him as Alex and Colin join us.

"Who's old?" Colin slaps me on the back before taking a seat next to me.

"No one said old."

"You called yourself old," Logan jests.

"Aww. Do you need some Icy Hot to get through the pain? I'm sure your grandma can spare some." Colin is laughing beside me.

"Seriously, how does Peyton keep you around sometimes?"

Colin quirks a brow at me. "Do you really want to know?"

I cringe. "No, I really don't."

"Thought so. She likes my big—"

"Please don't finish that sentence." Alex throws his hand up. "I love you both and really don't want to know."

Colin shakes his head. "I was going to say big personality. You two need to get your heads out of the gutter."

I roll my eyes. "Yes, because it's the two of us that are dirty-minded."

A ball is tossed into our circle, Colin grabbing it seamlessly out of the air.

"I was an innocent little football player when I joined this league. It's the two of you that corrupted me."

Laughter bursts out of me. "I needed a good laugh." I wipe a fake tear away from my eye. "I don't think you've ever been innocent."

Colin grins back at me, as Alex tries not to laugh. "This is me flipping you off in my head."

I return his smile. "Whatever you say, Colin. Whatever you say."

"Time to cut the chitchat, ladies." Frankie pops up out of nowhere behind me. "Fisher, I need you to run some of the stretches with Newman. He's a little tight today."

"Sure thing, Coach." My knees bend and crack as I stand.

"Don't want to keep her waiting." Alex waggles his brows at me. "You're already on her bad side."

"Wise words, Young."

Bad side, my ass. After the last few days together, I'm anything but on her bad side. I watch as she walks toward the rest of the defense, her ass looking delicious as ever in the joggers she's wearing.

I don't move fast, enjoying my view of her as I make my way over to Newman.

"How you feeling?" I ask, coming to stand next to him.

"Not bad."

"What hurts?"

"What doesn't hurt at this point?" he scoffs.

He's not wrong. At this point in the season, the aches and pains are constant and never really go away.

"Make sure you're taking time off from your workouts and see the trainers. Trust me, it's how I manage to get through the season at this point."

Rookies never want to admit when they're not feeling good. They don't want to be seen as weak because they don't want to be cut before making it to the regular season. I used to be like that. Pushing myself at every corner. Only after being in this league for years do I know how to take care of my body better.

Something I also learned from Frankie on that fateful night that we first hooked up.

Newman and I walk through our stretches as the stands start to fill up. Miami players are working out on the other side of the field. I recognize a few of them. Having been in the league for so long, you start to make friends with other players on other teams.

Maybe not friends, but acquaintances.

They are, after all, the only people who know what being in the league is like and the toll it takes on your body.

"Alright boys. Time to head in and get changed," Frankie calls out. A beanie is pulled down tight, her hair flowing down around her shoulders. Pink covers her face from the wind that's now blowing through the stadium.

She looks adorable as fuck.

I walk a step behind her as we head back toward the locker room. She's discussing the game plan with the linebackers coach.

There's nothing sexier than listening to her talk football. My high school girlfriend liked nothing more than wearing my jersey on spirit day. When I tried to talk about the game with her, her eyes would glaze over and I'd lose her.

Not Frankie.

There's a reason she got this job. The way she can command the linebackers with new players gets me going like nothing else.

It's like a drug, listening to her spout off about football.

I shove my hands in my sweatshirt pocket to try and keep my problem to myself. A wall of warmth hits me as I walk into the locker room.

Damn. It's a lot colder out than I thought. Going to make the hits land that much harder today.

"You ready to go, Knox?" Alex asks as I come back to my locker.

"Hell yeah. Going to be a good game."

"They've got a good new running back. Hear he's a beast."

I shake my head. "Won't be a problem for me."

"Better you than me. They said he can bench over three hundred pounds." Alex shakes his head. "He could run with you on his back."

I wave him off as I strip off my training clothes and pull on my pads. "I've got him covered."

"Watched all that film last night on him?" Colin pulls his jersey over his head.

"You know I did. Frankie demands perfection."

"You watch more film in a weekend than I do in a season," Colin says.

I give him a playful smile. "Maybe that means you should watch more film."

"Ouch." Colin drops his hand over his heart. "I take offense to that."

"Guess it means I'm the better player." I wink at him.

"Oooh. Those are fighting words," Logan says, looking back and forth between the two of us.

"You couldn't catch a touchdown pass." Colin crosses his arms. Alex is now standing between the two of us, his eyes bouncing around.

"We never did see if you could take down a three-hundred-pound linebacker."

"And I bet neither of you can kick a fifty-yard field goal

in thirty mile an hour winds," Jackson inserts. "Are you two still arguing about who's better?"

"Yes." We answer at the same time.

"Very mature," Alex says.

"I can't help it if I'm the best wide receiver in the league." Colin gives me that smug grin of his.

"Just like I can't help it that I'm the best linebacker in the league."

"Can we please be done with this pissing match?" Alex throws an arm over my shoulder. "You're both the best."

"What about me?" Logan asks. "Am I the best running back?" He bats his eyelashes at Alex.

"Fuck me. What in the world did you two start?" Alex whines.

"Not me." Colin points back at me. "Knox did."

"Gentlemen. If you don't mind, maybe you can finish your disagreement at some other time." Coach Brooks comes up behind us. "And here I thought Alex could keep you guys in line."

"They need a full time babysitter," he replies. "It's not going to be me."

"Well, let's get to it then."

Coach Brooks steps into the center of the locker room. Music from the stadium thumps through the space.

"It's going to be a tough game, Mountain Lions. Miami is a strong team this year. They've got a great new running back and he is not going to take it easy on us. Defense will have their hands full."

I look over to Colin, mouthing *good thing I'm the best*. He rolls his eyes back at me.

"We've got a strong offense and I know we will go out there and take care of business. Play hard. Play fast. Play smart. Let's head into the bye week with a win."

I take his place, stepping into the center of the fold.

The locker room is smaller here, built for soccer players and not football players with their oversized pads.

"You heard Coach," I bellow. "Play hard. Play fast. Family on three…one, two, three…"

"Family," echoes around me as we start to file out of the locker room and into the stadium. Defense runs out onto the field as the starting offense is announced.

The air is charged around us with excitement that kickoff is almost here. Even though we're considered the home team, neither team has an advantage here. Fans from all teams are represented today.

With a win today, the team will be sitting solidly in first place in the division.

Right where we want to be.

Alex, Colin, Jackson, and I head out toward midfield for the coin toss.

"Best of the best right here." Colin elbows me, giving me a huge grin.

"Damn fucking right." I match his smile. "No one else compares."

"Thank God this is over," Alex laughs as we meet Miami's players and shake hands.

Winning the coin toss, we defer to the second half and I get ready to take the field. There's nothing I love more than making a strong, defensive stop to start the game.

Our punter kicks off the game, the ball sailing right through the end zone as I grab my helmet and head onto the field.

Miami lines up. Their offense looks strong, standing in front of their quarterback and running back.

Alex wasn't kidding. This guy is huge. His biceps look like they are bigger than my thighs.

The ball is snapped and we all move. Safeties drop

back as I move toward the quarterback, spinning away from the guard. He gets the ball off before I get to him.

Their receiver doesn't make it far, our safeties dropping him three yards past the line of scrimmage.

This is what I love about our defense. All parts working together to stop them from moving down the field.

Two more stops and Miami is walking off the field. The crowd is roaring in delight.

"Great job, guys," Frankie is shouting at all of us as we head to the bench. "That was a great way to start the game." Her eyes move down the bench, locking on mine for a moment before moving on.

I didn't miss the twinkle there. She can't hide her pride at the execution of our plays.

Alex and the guys are marching down the field with ease. A throw here, a long run from Logan there and we're in the end zone.

"Hell yeah!" I pump a fist, reaching over to Newman for a high five.

"Alex makes it look easy."

He does. But we all know the amount of work he puts into his game. Except, for the first time, the game has taken a backseat for him. He's finally got someone to take his focus away from the game.

Not that anyone would know that. Now he just studies the film with Carter at his side.

The coach's son. Who would've ever guessed that?

I grab my helmet, getting ready to run back onto the field. Jackson nails the extra point.

"They're going to have cleaned up their mistakes on that first drive." Frankie huddles around us. "We're tight in the middle, but watch the sides."

I nod, jogging out to the field.

"Newman, watch the left." I call the play as Miami starts to scramble, changing the play at the line.

They move fast, snapping the ball and giving it to the running back. He's heading right to me. I lower my shoulder, ready to throw the hit to take him down.

But he's faster. Throwing all of his weight into me, he steamrolls right over. The force of the hit picks me up off my feet and slams me into the cold, hard, unforgiving ground.

It knocks the wind right out of me.

I fight to suck in a deep breath.

Fuck.

"Knox, you okay?" Newman appears above me. "That was a gnarly hit."

I roll into a sitting position, my back aching.

"Fuck."

Training staff comes out onto the field. Everything hurts.

I've taken some wicked hits before, but this one was no joke.

"How you feeling?" Paige, our trainer, drops down onto her knees in front of me.

"Just got the wind knocked out of me." I hold a hand out, and Newman helps me up. "I'm okay."

"We'll make sure. Bench."

I step over to the sideline more gingerly than I'd care to admit.

Damn. I really haven't taken a hit like this in a long time. One fall landing the wrong way and it can knock you out of the game for weeks.

"You okay?" Frankie asks as I walk past her. Her eyes are filled with concern.

"I'm fine."

The trainer directs me toward the blue medical tent. Helping me out of my pads, they inspect my ribs.

"Nothing feels broken," I tell the team doctor.

His hands are pushing on the affected area to check me over.

"We'll wrap it just to make sure."

By the time I'm suited back up again and out of the tent, Miami's tied the score. Fuck.

"You ready to go?" Frankie asks.

"All clear."

She studies me for a moment before turning back to the game. Our offense is back on the field, but can't make it past the thirty-yard line.

Frankie comes over to where I'm sitting on the bench next to Newman. "The run is working for them. You two are the first line of defense. Don't let them run wild over us today. Got it?"

"Got it," we both tell her.

Except that's exactly what they do. Miami runs the board all day. No matter what I do, I can't get to him. I can't take him down. Each missed hit has me getting up a tad slower. That first hit knocked me on my ass, and it's like I can't get back up to the level I'm used to playing at.

Our defense is no match for their running back. He shreds us for almost two hundred yards and two touchdowns.

Instead of leaving London with a win, we lose. 41-24.

It's embarrassing.

I let my team down. Now we have to head into the bye week with a loss.

Sometimes football really sucks.

# Chapter Seventeen

KNOX

"More bourbon, anyone?" Colin holds out the bottle to offer more to us. Everyone shakes their heads, but I hold out my glass. "Good man."

I'm going to need it if I'm going to make it through this night.

Standing here, with my closest friends and their partners, casts a glaring light that I'm the only single one left. I want to spend the night on Frankie's arm. To show her off to everyone, but I can't.

"Why didn't you want me to set you up with Ashley?" Tenley asks. "You guys would be so cute together."

"Tenley, leave the man alone." Jackson wraps an arm around her shoulders and pulls her in for a hug. "Let's enjoy our night out."

"Well, in that case, husband of mine…maybe we should enjoy the limo Colin got and have some bourbon."

"You two are not allowed to get frisky in the limo!" Colin points a finger at both of them. "Gross. Just gross."

"There's also five other people going with us, Colin." Peyton's voice is exasperated.

"Where is Logan tonight?" I ask, noticing he's still not here.

"He got a pass. Said he had to be back home sooner than he had wanted to." Peyton grabs her jacket and slips it on.

"Is everything okay?" I ask. Logan is more of a chatterbox than all these guys combined. It's not like him not to tell us.

"It's fine. He just had sad puppy dog eyes. Something about wanting to take his girlfriend home before her Olympic trials start."

"Aww. Who knew my girl was such a softie." Colin drops kisses all over her face.

"Knox, do you want to be his date tonight?" Peyton tries to push him off, but is laughing.

"I don't know if Colin could handle all of this." I wave a hand in front of me and send a wink his way.

"How do you put up with these egos?" Carter is smiling as he turns to Alex.

"It's because I have you to come home to." Alex drops a kiss on his lips.

"Is that what we look like?" Tenley whispers to Jackson, but we all hear it.

"You are all like this," I answer before anyone else can.

"Darlene really needs to find you someone. You need to get laid to release all this tension."

"If you only knew, Colin. If you only knew."

Except it's been a few weeks since Frankie and I have been together. We didn't hook up in London because our schedule was too tight.

Before that? When she took that hit.

It's like I've trained my body to look forward to Saturday nights. Every time we're together, it feels right. Like maybe we could be together for real.

But then she's yelling at me the next day from the sideline, and I know we can't.

No matter how much I want to be with her.

Colin goes to respond, but Peyton cuts him off. "Limo's here."

"Is there a reason you splurged for a limo tonight?" Alex asks, adjusting his tie as we all pile into the car.

"I didn't want anyone having to worry about getting home tonight."

"Smart." I settle into a seat, blowing out a sigh of relief. I'd gotten an X-ray of my ribs to ensure nothing is broken, but they're still a bit banged up.

The drive downtown to the Four Seasons where the event is being held is quick. We are raising money for the children's hospital in town, and the posh venue allows the organizers to charge more for the event and bring in big donors.

"Remember, you all need to be on your best behavior." Peyton eyes each one of us as we cram into the small elevator.

"Us?" I answer. "We're always on our best behavior."

"Sure." Peyton rolls her eyes at us. "Just don't make my job harder for me tomorrow."

"I'll make sure to keep these guys in line." Colin glares at all of us, stopping at me.

"What?" I throw my hands up as the elevator dings on our floor. "I'm not going to get in any trouble."

"Sure you won't." Colin slaps me as we all walk outside.

With the weather back to feeling more fall like, the event is being held outside on the pool deck. The noise of the city isn't as loud up here. String lights are hung all over. A thick, glass cover sits on top of the pool as people stand on top of it. Waiters are carrying around glasses of champagne and offer us each one. People in fancy suits and dresses mingle.

"Holy shit. This looks amazing, Peyton." Colin drops a kiss on her blushing cheeks.

"You've done a great job with this, Peyton. Really," Alex compliments her.

"Thank you. It wasn't all me."

"Don't let her fool you. She did it all," Colin says.

The guys delve into a conversation about how nice everything looks out here while my eyes stray. I know Frankie is coming tonight, but I haven't seen her.

I sip on my drink while I talk with people who come up and want to rehash the game from this past weekend.

I'm polite, thanking them for their tips on how I can hit better. The one downside of football fans—everyone thinks they know more than you.

Seeing Coach Jenkins, I make my way over to him.

"Fisher. How are the ribs feeling?"

"Fine."

He laughs. "Just like a football player. Won't tell people how you really feel."

"They'll be good as new after the bye week."

"What will be good as new?"

Frankie's smooth voice hits me and I spin around to see her.

Holy. Fuck.

I don't think I've ever seen her look more beautiful. Her hair falls down her shoulders in curls. Her face is all done up and she's wearing a red dress that clings to her every curve.

"His ribs." Coach Jenkins elbows me in the side, bringing me back to the present.

*I hope I'm not drooling.*

Because fuck. I cannot get over how sexy Frankie looks right now.

"Are they still bothering you?" Frankie asks, holding a glass of champagne in her hand.

"Like I told Coach here, they'll be good as new after the bye."

"As long as you rest." Frankie gives me a knowing look.

"Hey, I don't have any plans for the next week except to veg out on the couch."

"Now why don't I believe that?" Jenkins asks.

"Okay, maybe a few light workouts, but that's it."

My eyes drift back to Frankie. I can't get my fill of her. All I can think about is her in this dress.

I flip my gaze back to Jenkins, not wanting to be obvious in my perusal of her.

"Did you guys hear the news?" One of the other coaches comes up to us.

"What news?" I finish off my drink and grab another from a passing waiter.

"New York fired their receivers coach."

"What happened to her?" Frankie asks.

Frankie would know it's another female coach, seeing as how there are only three in the league total.

Well, two now.

"She was caught sleeping with one of her players."

Fuck. This can't be good.

"She was?" I don't miss the way Frankie's voice changes.

"Caused quite the scandal."

"I'm sure it did," Frankie mumbles.

I chance a quick glance at Frankie and she's white as a ghost.

"Good thing you don't have to worry about that,

Frankie." Jenkins elbows her in the side. "You're just one of the guys."

"Good thing." Her laugh is forced. She gulps down the rest of her drink. "I'm going to grab another. If you guys will excuse me."

She disappears faster than I've ever seen.

"What happened to the player?" I ask.

"What do you think happened? Nothing. Or if something did happen, they aren't telling us."

Fucking double standard. I can't imagine what is going through Frankie's mind right now.

"I'm going to go find another drink."

"Make sure to rest." Coach Jenkins points at me as I walk away.

"You got it."

Before I can take off to find Frankie, Alex and Carter corner me.

"You doing okay?"

"What? I'm fine."

Even I can tell my voice has too much bite to it.

"You've been off all night," Alex comments.

A swish of red fills my vision behind them. She's heading inside.

"Maybe I've had too much champagne."

"You might want to take it easy this weekend," Alex tells me. "You're always welcome to come watch the games with us."

"He is?" Carter asks. There's a quiet exchange between the two of them.

"Don't worry, I'm not going to take you up on that. I'm heading to the mountains for a few days."

"That sounds like more fun than hanging out with us." Carter laughs.

"It's a good way to clear my head."

A waiter breezes by us without stopping. I take that as my cue. "I'm going to go grab another drink. I'll catch up with you guys in a few."

I don't wait to hear their reply. Finding a break in the crowds, I duck inside the hotel.

Fuck. I have no idea where Frankie went.

I pace outside the elevators, trying to think. It's then I spot her coming out of a door at the end of the hallway. I run toward her. As soon as her eyes spot me, they widen in fear.

Backing her up toward the door, I push it open into the stairwell.

"What do you think you're doing?" Her whispered words are angry as the door slams shut behind me, echoing around us.

"Why are you avoiding me?" I back her up against the wall, dropping my hands on either side of her head.

"I'm not avoiding you."

"You ran out of there like you couldn't get away fast enough," I growl.

"You heard what they said." She points back to where we just came from.

"And? They're not us."

She huffs, shaking her head as she levels those fierce eyes on me. In her heels, she's as tall as I am.

"Knox, I'm too old for you."

"Bullshit."

"I'm seven years older than you. You can't deny it'd be easier with someone your own age."

"That's crap and you know it," I argue.

She keeps shaking her head. "But it's true. My focus is football. Yours should be too."

"Pretty sure that's the only thing we both focus on during the season."

"And what do you think is going to happen if people find out about us? C'mon, Knox, you're smarter than that."

"No one has found out yet."

"Yet being the keyword."

There's a bitterness to her tone that I don't like.

"So what are you suggesting then?"

I sweep a stray curl behind her shoulder. Goose bumps break out over her skin at my touch.

Whatever is going through her head right now, she can't deny how I make her feel. It's plain as day.

"Maybe we need to cool things off until the dust settles after that scandal."

"Fuck no."

It's already been too long without her. If I had known the Chicago game would've been the last time, hell, I would have savored each second with her.

I'm not ready for this thing to be done. Not even close.

"I'm your coach, Knox. Never mind the fact that I'm older than you—"

"Doesn't matter," I cut her off.

Her fingers come up to massage her temple, like this whole evening is giving her a headache. I can feel her brain working a mile a minute, trying to come up with every excuse in the book as to why this won't work. "Knox..."

"Go away with me this weekend."

Her laugh is empty as it escapes her. "That's the last thing we need to be doing."

"I'm serious. Get away from everything in Denver. The team. The news. It'll just be us."

"I don't know if that's a good idea."

"Frankie, please," I plea.

This thing between us? It was supposed to be a fling. A way to burn off energy during the season.

I'm so far past a fling, it's not even funny.

I want this woman with a burning desire I've never felt. And I'm not going to let her give up on us because of two people who couldn't practice discretion.

I step in closer to her. This time, her eyes aren't filled with anger, but a heat I'm familiar with. That I can work with.

"I know you're scared, but give me this weekend. Just you and me. If you don't want anything to do with me after that, fine."

I cup her cheek, swiping my thumb over her lips.

I don't want this to be the end. I'm so far gone for this woman. But if she says no, I'll live with it. How? I don't want to entertain that idea.

"Okay."

I blow out a breath, dropping my forehead to hers.

"Then be at my house tomorrow morning."

I drop a quick kiss on her lips and step back.

"Okay."

"I promise, it'll be okay."

I push out of the doors and head back toward the event.

I only hope I can make good on my promise.

Because if I can't, I don't know what I'm going to do without her.

# Chapter Eighteen

## FRANKIE

Out of all the ways I thought I'd be spending my bye week, this wasn't it. Panicking at the last minute at Knox's front door as my rideshare drives away.

We've never done anything like this before.

But after hearing the need in his voice last night, I couldn't deny him. Or myself. Even though every voice in my head is screaming at me that I'll be next. That someone will find out about us and I'll be fired.

I go to knock on the door, but it swings open.

Knox leans against the frame, his smile easy. He's wearing a black sweatshirt and jeans. His hair is wet from the shower. Easy and casual.

How he always is.

"You were going to cancel, weren't you?"

"No I wasn't."

"Sure you weren't."

Taking the bag from my hand, I follow Knox through his house. I've never been here before.

I expected big and modern, but it's homey. Like it's had a woman's touch. Oversized couches, no doubt to fit

Knox's hulking form, are lined with pillows and blankets. Pictures line the bookshelves on either side of the TV.

It opens straight into the kitchen that Knox is walking through. It isn't the most modern, but looks well used, something that surprises me for a football player. Most guys get their meals through a service. But not the man in front of me.

"Where are we going?" I change the subject. I hate how well Knox knows me. But it's not like we haven't been doing this thing together for a few years.

"I have a little cabin in the woods."

I fight the groan. After how hard this season has been, a cabin in the woods with Knox?

Sounds like the best damn thing in the world.

"Then what are we waiting for?"

Knox gives me his panty-melting smile. The one that makes me want to jump his bones.

But I don't.

Because I want to spend the weekend with him in the woods.

After the loss on Sunday, I could see how much he carried the weight of it. Losing to any team is hard. Playing in a completely new environment in London didn't help. Knox was playing through pain because he didn't want to let his team down.

It's one of the many reasons we connected so easily. We both have a hunger for the game. To give it our all.

Really, we just love football.

"You coming?" Knox is standing inside another door-way, to what I'm only assuming is his garage.

"Waiting on you." I pat his chest as I walk by.

Knox hurries past me, opens the passenger door to his truck, and I climb in.

"I've been waiting on you for a long time."

He shuts the door before I can respond.

I watch as he walks around the front of the black truck and hops in.

"Music?" Knox fiddles with the radio.

"Whatever is fine."

A rock song blasts through the speakers as we head out. It's like neither one of us knows how to be with each other like this. We're always surrounded by football, but not this time.

Even in London, we were there because of the game.

Knox's fingers drum on the steering wheel in time with the beat of the music.

"So…"

"This is weird."

We both say at the same time.

I blow out a breath, relieved I'm not the only one feeling nervous. "You feel weirded out by this too?"

Knox chances a glance at me before swinging his attention back to the road. He flips on his blinker to merge onto the highway, heading west out of the city.

"I mean, it's kind of new. Going away together?"

I nod, even though he isn't looking my way. "I'm definitely not counting all of our away games."

"Would it make you feel better to have me run sprints?"

I reach across the center console and slap him on the arm. "I am not that bad!"

"Eh, according to the guys you are the worst."

I laugh. "Do they really believe you're that bad of a player?"

"Nah. They just think I can't keep my mouth shut and keep getting in trouble."

"I mean, you can run your mouth."

"You love my mouth."

I see the smirk playing at the corner of his lips. "Irrelevant. What I don't get is how the guys can think you'd still be on the team if you are that much of a troublemaker."

"I'm only a troublemaker for you."

"You've been a pain in my ass since the first day you started."

"Oh God, I was such a tool." Knox drags a hand down his face.

"You thought Coach Jenkins was me. That was priceless."

"I hope I'm not still that much of a tool."

"Some days." I rest my elbow on the console, dropping my chin in my hand and turning my attention to him.

"Are you always this cheeky?" Knox reaches across and squeezes my thigh.

"Someone needs to keep you in check."

"Good thing I have you then."

Just like that, the awkwardness breaks. The drive into the mountains is easy. With it being this late in October, the aspen trees aren't in bloom, but it's still beautiful.

Knox pulls off the highway and goes higher into the mountains. After passing a few cabins, we pull into the driveway of one that looks out over a sparkling lake below.

"This place is huge." Awe fills my voice as I stare up at what can only be classified as a log mansion.

"It's all they had available."

Knox stops and I hop out of the truck. Fresh mountain air hits me. I suck in a deep breath, pushing every negative thought out of my mind. It's a clear day, fluffy white clouds dotting the sky.

"It could be worse, that's for sure."

Knox walks around the truck, holding his hand out to me. "Want to go see it?"

I link my hand with his and follow him to the house. A

wide porch with rocking chairs lines the front. Glass doors open up into a huge, two-story living room that backs up to the forest. Wood panels line the walls. A shag rug sits in front of the fireplace.

"Wow. This is pretty incredible."

Toeing off my shoes, I sink my bare feet into the rug. Knox is grinning back at me.

"I'm glad you approve."

"Where are the bedrooms?"

"Which one?"

Spotting the stairs at the other side of the living room, I run toward them, Knox hot on my heels. I head for the closed door at the end of the hallway. Pushing it open, I come to a dead stop.

"Umm, Knox?"

"What is it?"

His muscular chest comes up behind me.

"Did you mean for this to be a romantic retreat?" I shift to see his eyes taking in the room in front of us.

"Fuck."

Rose petals cover the bed as two towels, folded into the shape of swans, kiss each other. A bottle of champagne is sitting on ice next to the window with chocolate-covered strawberries on the tray.

"Holy shit. I said I was coming for a getaway. Apparently they took it to mean a completely different kind of getaway."

Knox looks absolutely horrified at the sight of love exploding all over the room. It has laughter burbling out of me. "I mean, we shouldn't let it go to waste, right?"

Stepping to the window, Knox pulls out the champagne. "You're right. I'm sure they're charging me way too much money for this."

I walk over to him, my bare toes touching his sock-clad

feet. I grab a glass and hold it out to him. "Then pour me one. This looks like the good stuff."

Knox smirks as he pops the bottle, letting fizz rush down into my glass.

"Should we toast?"

Knox smiles at me. "That's usually Alex's thing."

"Fine then." I hold my glass up to his. "To the bye week. Hopefully you can put the loss behind you and look forward to the next game."

"Cheers to that." We clink and I sip on the champagne, bubbles exploding on my tongue.

"What all did you have planned for this weekend?" I take a step closer to the window.

"Whatever you want to do." I don't miss the heat in his voice.

"I thought you wanted to just get away and relax."

Knox grabs my glass and sets it down. "Relaxation can take many forms, Frankie."

"Oh yeah?" Crossing my arms, I fix my gaze to Knox.

"Do you need me to teach you how to relax?" Knox takes a step closer.

I shrug a shoulder. "I could use a lesson."

Without warning, Knox grabs me around the waist and tackles me onto the bed in an explosion of rose petals.

"What are you doing?" I shout, laughter escaping me.

"We're relaxing."

"You're going to scare the swans."

Knox looks down at the towel birds, grabbing one and throwing it off the end of the bed. "Better?"

"Yes. Now, how about those relaxation lessons?"

# Chapter Nineteen

KNOX

Every body part cracks as I wake up. Frankie sits in the bed next to me, my T-shirt stretched across her legs. An iPad plays on her lap with footage from our next opponent.

"Do you ever stop?" My voice is sleepy as I roll toward her, draping an arm around her waist.

"If you didn't sleep so long…"

"Maybe if you didn't wear me out last night."

Frankie tosses the iPad to the side and flips on her side to face me. Pillow creases cut across her face. This is something I don't get. I don't get mornings with Frankie.

When we're together, it's only for the night.

We fuck and then we go our separate ways.

Do I hate it?

Yes.

Do I have to live with it because we can't be more?

Yes.

"That would require you staying up past eight."

"You try taking the hit I did on Sunday and then sitting on a plane for ten hours."

Frankie's fingers play with the chain that rests on my chest. "Do you need a little TLC?"

"If I whine and complain, will you help?" I stick out my bottom lip like a pouty toddler. Frankie only grins back at me.

"You don't have to whine and complain." She pulls my shoulder down. "Lie down and I'll help."

"I thought I'd have to grovel." I laugh into the pillow as I adjust myself on the bed.

"I saw the hit you took. Hell, after taking one myself, you can just ask."

Frankie straddles my ass, her hands now resting on my back. It's the briefest touch, but it sets my body on fire.

"I love playing D, but at this point in the season, it gets harder and harder to rebound at my age."

Frankie digs her fists into my shoulders. Fuck, does that feel amazing.

"Yes, being twenty-seven is so hard."

"Hey." I reach around and pinch her thigh. "Not all of us age as well as you do."

"Yes, you're really showing your age, Knox. This fine physique of yours has everyone talking about how terrible it is to age."

Frankie moves her hands down my back, thumbs working over the sore muscles. "If football doesn't work out, you could always get a career as a massage therapist."

"Don't even put that out in the universe. I don't want to jinx it."

"You have nothing to worry about. I've seen you on the field with the guys."

Her hands pause on my back. "I wish it were that simple," she sighs.

I roll under her so I can face her. "Are you still worrying about that other coach?"

Her hands go to my chest, now tracing the tattoo on my pec.

"Of course I am. I have to work twice as hard to prove myself because I'm a woman. You saw how easily they dropped her."

I growl. "You know more about football than most of the team. I don't see how they can just get rid of you."

She shrugs a shoulder. "It is what it is."

I hate how defeated she sounds. Instead of this being a relaxing time away, the first morning, we're diving right into the heavy stuff. "That really makes me want to punch someone." I drag my hands up her thighs, resting them under the hem of her shirt.

"I don't need you fighting on my behalf. It would probably make the situation worse."

"Maybe I can send Newman in then. He still has a baby face. People can't say no to him."

Frankie laughs, a deep belly laugh that hits me square in the gut. "He is very easy to say no to."

"What about me?"

A devious smile cuts across her face. "You want me to tell you no?"

"Apparently it's easy to tell me no."

"I think you believe you can charm your way into anything with me."

Grabbing her hips, I flip us so I'm now on top of her. Honey-brown hair spreads out on the pillow. The sun, now peeking through the trees, casts shadows over Frankie.

My heart catches in my chest. It hits me like a freight train.

Frankie's smile. The way I got to wake up next to her this morning. How easy it is between the two of us when it's only us. The way she didn't hesitate to take care of me right now.

Fuck, I love this woman.

I know she has her hesitations about the two of us. She's older than I am. She's my coach. I'm sure she could think of a million other reasons why we shouldn't be together.

This has been a lot more for a long time now. It started out as a way to blow off steam during the regular season.

Seeing as how we had the same schedules, it was easy. A quick fuck here or there. Over the years, my need for her has grown to something I can't suppress. It's a living, breathing thing inside of me.

Today was the first time I've ever gotten to wake up next to her. To feel her soft curves in the morning is how I want to start every day. To see her in my T-shirt and nothing else.

But until the reality of our situation changes, it's more stolen nights.

"You went quiet. Are you trying to think of a way to charm me?" Frankie drags a finger over the furrow in my brow.

"Maybe we could have our coffee outside."

She beams at me. "No."

"No?"

"See? It's very easy for me to tell you no."

I tickle her right side, knowing full well it's the only place she's ticklish. "Did you have something else in mind then?"

"I just wanted to tell you no." She's squirming beneath me.

I settle my weight over her, my forehead kissing hers. "What am I going to do with you?"

"Hmm, maybe make us breakfast and then we can eat outside."

I nip at her bottom lip. "You drive me crazy."

"So you've told me." Frankie wraps her hands around my neck, playing in the ends of my hair.

"I don't know why I keep you around."

Except I do.

"You need someone to knock you down a peg. To keep your big football ego in check."

"I wasn't aware I had one."

"Oh, you don't. But that's only because of me."

"Because you tell me no." I shake my head.

"Exactly. You wouldn't like it if I agreed with you all the time."

"Maybe once or twice wouldn't kill you," I grumble.

Frankie kisses the corner of my mouth. "How about breakfast?" She drops a kiss to the other side of my mouth. It has my dick getting hard. "And then maybe we can find an activity that we both agree on?"

"I'll agree to that."

# Chapter Twenty

## FRANKIE

Dark clouds have been rolling in all afternoon. After breakfast, Knox fell asleep and I curled up in front of a roaring fire.

It's been the perfect afternoon. I haven't thought about football once.

"What are you doing?"

Knox's voice from behind startles me.

"Jesus, you scared the shit out of me."

He smirks. "Why are you so jumpy?"

I hold up the book in my hand. "It's a thriller."

Knox flips it to see the cover.

"Are you using this as a guide?"

"I'm sorry, a guide for what?"

Knox bends over the back of the couch. His face is scruffier than normal.

"Are you going to try and kill me in my sleep?"

Reaching behind him, I pull him over the couch.

"Yes. That's exactly what I plan on doing. You better sleep with one eye open."

"Damn, Frankie. And here I thought you liked me."

"Eh."

Knox grabs the book out of my hand and flips to the page I was on. Rain starts coming down. "This guy kills someone with a straw? That seems unreasonable."

"Do you always have to be so critical of the things I like?"

"What am I being critical of?" A playful grin is on his face.

"You were judgy about my movie."

"What eighteen-year-old goes off to London on their own? It's not possible."

I run a hand through his messy hair. "Have you always been like this?"

He gives me a smug smile. "According to my mom and grandma, yes."

"Believe you me, if I wanted to off you, all I'd have to do is lace donuts with poison. You never say no to donuts when they bring them in after practice."

Knox looks affronted. "Have you ever had VooDoo donuts? They are the best damn things in the world."

"I know. That's why you'd make it really easy to kill you."

His brows furrow together. "I don't really like where this conversation is going."

"Then maybe I should pick apart the things you like."

"Isn't that what you do on a weekly basis?"

"I prefer to call it coaching…"

"Why'd you decide to go into coaching?" Knox's brown eyes gleam up at me.

"That's random."

"I don't think I've ever heard the story."

"It was nothing exciting. I went to practice with my older brother a few times and fell in love. And then when my little brother decided to play, I was already working with my college's football team and helping him run plays."

"You didn't do it because you thought the football players were cute?"

I laugh. "That was probably the reason I kept going back with my brother."

"Damn. I was only kidding."

"Hey!" I smack him on the chest. "I was in high school. Give a girl a break."

"I'm sorry. I'm trying to picture it. I just can't picture you fawning all over other players when I've seen you make Newman cry."

I roll my eyes. "I didn't make him cry."

"You made him cry."

"At least you know he's in it for the long haul."

"I don't think football's made me cry since my grandpa took me to my first practice."

"It made you cry?" My fingers are playing with his hair. "Now that's something I find hard to believe."

"It did!" he defends. "I was seven. I got hit so hard, I ran off the field and barely made it under the stands before I started crying."

"And you kept playing?"

"My grandpa told me if I could take a hit like that, it would get easier."

"And did it?"

He laughs. "Fuck no. It only got harder, but at least I knew what was coming."

"You should really do yoga. It helps."

"How do you know?" Knox readjusts himself, turning to face me head-on. His hand finds my free one and links our fingers.

"Yoga is good for you. Helps keep you limber."

"Maybe you can show me your moves."

"All in the hips." I wink at him.

Knox groans, closing his eyes. "You really are trying to kill me."

"Not today, I'm not."

"If you try to teach me yoga, you will."

"Duly noted. Just like if I ever try to cook for you, I'll probably kill you."

"You don't know how to cook?" Knox's hand stops playing with mine.

I shake my head. "Not in the least. My parents were terrible cooks, so it was not a skill that was passed down."

Knox hops up off the couch. "How about an early dinner then?"

"You're going to cook for me?"

"Oh yeah. I'm kind of awesome at it."

"Look at you with the hidden skills."

He shrugs a shoulder. "I don't get to do it often, so I like getting to do it."

"Good point."

"My grandma taught me. I think she was convinced I would die my first year in Denver if I didn't know how."

"That's amazing," I say on a laugh.

Knox drops a quick kiss on my lips.

"Then sit back, relax, and let me amaze you some more."

"SERIOUSLY, WHAT SMELLS SO GOOD?"

After Knox told me he was going to make dinner, I dozed off on the couch. Between the fire and the rain pattering against the window, it lulled me into a blissful sleep.

And now I get to wake up to the sexiest man making dinner for me.

"It's a recipe from my grandma. It's easy to make and as she said, 'something a bonehead like me couldn't screw up.'"

I try to cover my mouth to stop the laugh from bursting out, but it doesn't work. "Your grandma is kind of the best."

Knox rolls his eyes. "Somedays. She never let me get a big head for being in the league."

"I don't think anyone could ever accuse you of having a big head." I study the man in front of me. He's more relaxed than I've ever seen him. During the season, everything is always amped up. The adrenaline is never-ending because the guys always have to be ready for anything that might be tossed their way.

"I'm glad you think so."

I sip the red wine that Knox poured for me while I sit and watch him cook.

*This is something that I could get used to.*

"Coach Brooks wouldn't let anyone who plays for him have a big head," I state.

"Even Colin who probably had the biggest head of all. Telling everyone he played for Denver to get them into bed."

"You mean you never used that line?" I laugh it off, but now I'm curious. It's something we've never talked about. When we started this thing, we made it so that we were exclusive to each other. Before that? I didn't want to know.

"Hell no."

"Please." I gulp down the rest of my wine.

Knox drops the lid on the pan and stalks over to me. Grabbing my chair, he spins me so I'm facing him. He leans over me, his clean scent overwhelming. There's a heated look in my eye.

"Believe me when I say this, Francesca." God, just the sound of my name sends tingles shooting through me. "I have never used my status to get any woman. Not when the only woman I've wanted is right here in front of me."

I don't think. I lean up and capture Knox's lips in a passionate kiss. His hands find my hair and hold on tight. He nips at my bottom lip, and I relish the sting. Our tongues tease one another. It has need drawing up tighter in every nerve of my body.

Knox takes control, slowing us down. My hands fist in his shirt to keep him close. I'm not sure who is moaning louder—him or me. But this kiss is everything I love about this man wrapped up in a neat, tiny package.

Commanding yet deliberate.

Powerful yet soft.

All too soon, Knox pulls back. His eyes are half-lidded and his lips swollen. I bite my lip as I lean in closer to him.

"Don't ever doubt me, Frankie. I'll prove you wrong every time."

He drops a quick peck on my lips before returning to the stove.

A flush creeps up my neck at his words. "Is that how you'll prove me wrong?"

Thinking about that kiss has my toes curling. No man has ever made me feel this way. How very inconvenient for me that he's my player.

"One of the ways." Knox winks at me.

Butterflies threaten to erupt out of me as Knox plates the chicken and walks toward me.

"Now, you need to eat up because I have plans for you tonight."

Knox sits beside me, pulling my legs up into his lap.

His fingers dance up and down my leg as he digs into the meal.

I grab a hearty bite. Flavors explode on my tongue as I greedily take another bite. The lemon and garlic mixed together is sinful in how good it is. "This is delicious," I say, very unladylike with a large piece in my mouth.

Knox smirks at me. "I knew you'd like it."

"Thank God your grandma taught you to cook. I'm useless in the kitchen."

"Maybe you should keep me around then."

I smile at him. I want to tell him I'll keep him around, but the weight of what happened to the coach in New York is still heavy on my mind.

That could have easily been me. I saw the pictures. I know they were careless. All it takes is one wrong step and our secret is out there. The fact that I'm his coach is bad enough, but people might think I forced him into this thing because I'm older.

Which is the furthest thing from the truth.

Knox doesn't need an answer from me.

"Thank you for coming out here with me," he tells me.

"I'm glad it worked out." I shrug, like it's no big deal.

"I'm serious." He grabs my hand, linking our fingers together. "I know it's been a shitty week for both of us, so I'm glad you came."

I squeeze his hand. "You're such a cerebral player. Sometimes you get too in your head and get in your own way."

"It's hard not to when the game is your entire life."

Dropping my fork, I scoot over onto Knox's lap. My hands find his head and start rubbing his scalp. He moans in delight.

"That's why you need to escape sometimes. Leave football behind and just be in the present."

"Says the coach."

"Hey." I drop a kiss on his temple before sinking my hands into his hair again. "I love football, and even I need a break from it every now and again."

Knox wraps his arms around me and relaxes into my touch. His soft whimpers and moans tell me he's enjoying this.

I love being the one to bring him comfort. This thing between us is hard. There are times where I want to run to him and make sure he's okay, but I can't. I want to be with him, but our jobs are on the line. My promotion.

Maybe one day, when he's no longer playing, we could make this work. But can we live in the shadows until that day?

"Why'd you stop?" Knox whispers against my neck.

"Sorry."

Knox looks up at me, eyes tired. "Is it too soon to go to bed?"

I smile at him, trying to hide my sadness at the thought of never being with him like I want to. My mind keeps trying to find a way to make this work, but I'm not seeing one that won't end up with me losing my job.

Standing, I link his hand with mine. I don't care about dinner anymore. All I want is to be with Knox.

He follows as I lead us upstairs to our room. As soon as I spin to face him, he's lifting me into his arms and settling on the bed.

Our kisses are urgent. There's a need to this that I haven't felt before. It's almost like we can both sense that there's a time crunch on this.

I don't waste another second, reaching into Knox's sweats and finding his hard length.

"Fuck, I love your hands on me."

Pushing Knox off of me and onto his back, I move down the bed so I can take him into my mouth.

He thrusts up into me the moment my lips wrap around the head of his cock. His words are gibberish as I suck him to the back of my throat. My hand strokes down, playing with his balls. The salty taste of precum hits my tongue, causing heat to gather between my legs.

"You're way too good at that, Frankie." Need laces his voice. "I don't want to come down your throat."

"Where do you want to come, then?" I pop off him, my hand still moving on him.

"Fuck. I need to be inside you."

We make quick work of our clothes, our hands moving back onto one another. It's like if we're not touching, one of us will disappear.

Leaning back against the headboard, Knox pulls me to him. His hands tangle in my hair as he brings me in for another kiss.

I can't get close enough to him. I drink in everything he is giving me as I sink down onto him. He swallows my gasps as I settle over him.

Each thrust, every rock, is hurried. We move in tandem. Desire is coursing through me. I can't get to my orgasm fast enough. Knox holds me to him. Nothing could get between the two of us. Our eyes lock.

The connection between the two of us is something I've never felt. It should scare me. But as it pushes me over the edge, I welcome it. My orgasm pulls Knox's out of him.

Every piece of me settles as we come down from this high together. This thing with Knox is everything. I want it with every fiber of my being.

He gave me the option to back out after this weekend. But now?

How could I?

Whatever passed between the two of us tonight has pushed every foreboding thought to the back of my mind.

I'm his coach? Doesn't matter.

I'm too old? Not even a blip on the radar.

All because of the man holding me in his arms like I'm something to be cherished.

All because of Knox.

"Are you okay?" Knox's words are whispered.

I shift, looking him dead in the eyes. I want him to understand this.

"I'm all in, Knox."

"You are?" Surprise lights up his face.

"All in. You and me."

"That sounds pretty damn good."

Yeah, it really does.

# Chapter Twenty-One

### FRANKIE

"Becky! I'm so happy you could make it." I wrap my friend up in a hug.

"I wouldn't miss this game for the world."

"Really?" I quirk a brow in her direction.

"Okay, fine. It worked out that I wasn't scheduled to work today."

I laugh. "It's okay. I know you don't like football."

"No, but I do like the players." She eyes everyone out on the field.

While families usually come to the games, they don't come out onto the field. After the loss in London, management thought it might be fun to change the mojo and have them on the field during warm-ups.

And because my family isn't local, Becky is the next best thing.

"Hey Coach, who's your friend?" Newman comes up to us.

"Aren't you adorable?" Becky gushes at him.

"Ryan Newman." He extends his hand out to her.

"Happily married Becky." He blushes as she takes his hand. "I'm way too old for you."

"Age is only a number." He winks before running back to where Knox is watching us.

"Who's Mr. Broody over there?" Becky steps closer.

I'm not involved with the guys during warm-ups unless they need me. I can feel Knox's stare from here.

"Knox Fisher. Pain in my ass linebacker."

"Oh honey, he might be a pain, but hopefully the pleasurable kind."

"What is this I hear…you two ladies talking about pleasure?"

I spin around to see Knox's grandma standing behind us. "Darlene. Hi!" I go up and try to shake her hand, but she pulls me in for a hug instead.

"It's wonderful to see you again, dear."

"You too. I take it you had a good time in London?"

"Oh, it was fabulous. Knox spoiled us the whole time. But you know how wonderful he is."

"Umm…" Becky's eyes are glued to mine as the man in question runs up to us.

"Grandma, hi." He leans down to press a kiss to her cheek.

"Hi, my sweet boy. I was just saying hi to Frankie and her friend here."

"Becky." She sticks her hand out for both of them to shake.

"I don't think I've met any of your friends before," Knox comments.

"It's not like I see this one very often." Becky points at me. "If it's not football, it's not on her radar."

"Hey. I'm not that bad."

"Knox is the same way," Darlene interjects.

"I'm glad it's not just me then. All this football talk and my eyes glaze over."

"There's more to life than football."

The two of them start going back and forth, ignoring Knox and me.

"Do you feel ganged up on?" I ask him.

"We don't only talk about football," Knox grunts.

Football was the furthest thing from our minds the last weekend, but they can't know that. Hell, the last few times Knox and I have been together, football hasn't come up. It's been just the two of us enjoying each other's company.

"Will we be watching the game together, Becky?" Darlene asks her.

"I think we will be." They link arms, waving at the two of us and walking through the tunnel where other families are heading for their seats.

"Okay, is it weird they like each other?" Knox asks.

"Very."

Knox and I have always kept our lives separate. It was one of my rules when we started this thing. Less messy.

To see two important people to us hang out like this?

It's weird.

"I feel like they're going to gang up on us," I tell him.

"I really don't like the looks on their faces." They turn back to us one more time before disappearing.

"Guess that means I need a new best friend."

Knox snorts behind me. "I can't give up my grandma."

"She'd kill you if you did that."

"If I ever go mysteriously missing, you'll know why," he says with a laugh.

"Aww, I'm sure you'll be missed."

"See,"—Knox turns to me—"your tone doesn't say that."

I stick out my bottom lip. "Poor Knoxy. Worried you're not feeling loved?"

"Loved, huh?"

I want to pull the word back the moment it comes out.

This can't possibly be love.

Sure, I felt a deeper connection being away with Knox, but it can't be love.

I finally got out of my head about him, and now love?

Can it really be love?

"Why does Knox get out of warm-ups?" Newman comes up, complaining. Thank God, because he breaks the awkward tension at my silence at Knox's words.

Newman's running through normal pregame warm-ups, but will sit today because of a pulled quad muscle during practice this week.

"You need to stretch that leg of yours. I'm all warmed up. But if you want to do some suicide drills, I'm happy to do them with you."

"Never mind." He flees in the wake of not wanting to do the worst drills we have.

"You're mean."

"Kid needs to learn." Knox backs away from me, heading back toward his teammates. "Is it bad I'm already looking forward to the next game?"

My body lights up at the thought, even if I'm now warring with myself about what I'm feeling toward this man.

"Not as much as I am."

# Chapter Twenty-Two

"You should've seen him. Before you know it, he'll be kicking a football," Jackson gushes. Mondays are always easy days after a win. Between that and the time off during the bye, the guys are feeling good.

Now, with no set practice after a win, the guys and I usually come to the weight room for some light training.

"No way. He's going to be catching passes like Uncle Colin."

"Noah kicked a soccer ball and you already have him starting for the Mountain Lions?" I ask Jackson. Pushing the weight bar up, I set it in the resting spot and sit up. "What if he doesn't like football?"

Four sets of eyes glare at me.

"Why would you even say that?" Logan asks. "That's blasphemy."

A sly grin spreads across my face. "You guys are always saying as long as your kids are happy, you don't care about that stuff. Just sayin'." It's just too easy to mess with them.

"They'll like football." Jackson is matter-of-fact about it

as he continues with his own workout. "How can someone not like football?"

I shrug a shoulder. "Beats the fuck out of me. It's the best game in the world."

"Like, what do you do on Sundays if you don't watch football?" Colin asks. "I'd be so bored."

"It's a good thing we will never have to figure that out," Alex says, taking a swig of water. "Speaking of kids…"

"Any news?" I ask.

Alex is grinning like an idiot, so whatever it is, it's good news. "Our surrogate is pregnant."

"Holy shit!" Colin jumps up, wrapping his arms around him. We all follow suit, giving him huge hugs.

"You're going to be a dad?" I ask.

He nods, his eyes wet with tears. "I can't believe it happened this fast. Thank God Carter knew someone, or who knows where we'd be."

"Noah will have someone to play with. We need more kids around here." Jackson looks over at Colin and me.

"Hey, don't include me in that," Colin says. "Peyton and I are happy with Waffles."

"I don't have anyone to have kids with," I defend.

I've never really even thought about having kids. It's never been on my radar. Even this thing with Frankie is limited because it's only during the season. And it's not like it's something we talk about.

"That's great news, man," Logan inserts. "Raising the second generation of the Mountain Lions."

"If they like football…"

"Really, Knox?"

I laugh. "You guys are just too easy."

"Fisher. Need you in the meeting room." Coach Riley, the defensive coordinator, pops his head into the weight room.

"Oooh. He must have heard you don't like football. Someone's in trouble now," Colin jests.

"Nah. It's not Frankie. He'll be fine," Alex replies as I grab a water bottle and head out of the room.

There's a tingling in my gut. I don't know what caused this spur-of-the-moment meeting, but I try not to focus on everything it could be about.

Like someone finding out about me and Frankie.

Except wouldn't Coach Brooks be the one to yell at me about that?

Pushing the worry aside, I head into the meeting room where Frankie and the linebackers coach are waiting with someone I don't recognize. His presence is imposing. With thick biceps and short hair, the lack of smile makes him look menacing.

Not someone I'd want to cross paths with outside of the game. And I'm not easily intimidated.

"Sorry to disrupt your weight training, Knox, but we have someone you need to meet." Coach Jenkins welcomes me into the room.

My eyes shift around the room, taking in the easy posture of the two coaches. Frankie's isn't as easy. She looks more stiff.

"Knox, this is Lucas Black. He's joining the team as one of our newest linebackers."

"Am I being cut?" A lead weight drops into my stomach.

Riley brushes me off. "Not at all. With some players going down, we needed to shift guys around, and Lucas here is an up-and-coming star."

He nods to me. "Sup."

*Sup?*

Who does this kid think he is?

*Sup?*

My grandma would've smacked the crap out of me if I ever addressed someone new like that.

"Not a star yet." I manage to get my own jabs in.

I'm not stroking my own ego for the sake of it. I know the stats. My numbers are the highest in the league this season.

"Relax, Knox. No one is taking your job away from you. But we do need help with Newman going out for a few weeks."

I grind my jaw. I hate the thought of a new kid coming in and threatening my position and taking over.

I've worked my ass off to get where I am in this league. I never settled for being good enough. I always strived toward better.

The feeling of being replaced is one I'm all too familiar with. My dad left us and started his own new family. It made me feel second best and motivated me to work that much harder to never feel that way again.

Now, that feeling is spreading through me. I can't do a damn thing about it because if I don't, I'll surely be benched.

"Sure. Whatever it takes to help the team."

Riley claps me on the shoulder. "Good. Get outside. We're going to have Coach Rose run some drills with the defense."

Frankie gives him a grim nod as they all file out of the room. I don't miss the way that Lucas assesses me on his way out.

Fucker.

"Knox, don't." Frankie's voice is quiet as the door clicks shut behind us.

I turn on her. "You didn't think I deserved to know that they were bringing in a new linebacker?"

"I didn't know," she hisses. "I was told about five minutes before you found out."

"Fuck." I scrub a hand through my hair. "Is that guy really helping fill holes in the defense, or is my job on the line?"

"I didn't even know he was coming."

"Really?"

Frankie slams a hand down on the table. "Despite what you might think, I don't know everything that goes on. I'm not involved in the decision-making of the team because I'm still an assistant coach, Knox. I execute plays that are given to me. I have no say in what else goes on."

I want to throw something. Punch the wall. Anything to take out this anger that is swirling in my gut.

"It feels like I'm being replaced, Frankie." It slips out before I can rein it back in.

Frankie peers around me, making sure the door is closed before approaching me. The tips of her sneakers line up with mine.

"Knox. You are not being replaced." She squeezes my bicep before pulling away. "I promise you can trust Coach Riley; he was only brought in for backup while Newman recovers and Taylor is out in concussion protocol."

"You're sure?"

"Promise."

I stare down at her. Her words should be reassuring, but they are anything but. The dread is still there that this guy is going to be gunning for my position. Frankie gives me a comforting smile, her brown eyes soft.

"We should head out to the field." Frankie takes a step back. "You're one of the best players I've ever coached, Knox. Don't let this get in your head."

Too late.

Black has the guys laughing before I make it out on the field.

"Knox, have you met Lucas? He was just telling us this awesome story about a girl he hooked up with when he was playing in New York," one of the guys tells me.

"I'm sure it's hilarious," I bite out.

"You need my help?" Lucas claps me on the shoulder. "I've got skills on and off the field."

"I'm good." I push his arm off of me.

"See, I think you might need my help."

"Do I?" I cross my arms, practically glowering at him. What a dick.

"I've got more hits than you this season."

"No, you don't."

I know my stats. This guy is good, but not as good as I am.

"More forced fumbles."

"What, do you want a fucking ribbon for doing your job?" My patience is running thin with this guy.

"You guys done chatting? Or do you need a few more minutes before we can start practice?" Frankie's voice barks out at us.

Lucas nods in Frankie's direction as the rest of the guys start lining up.

"What's her story?"

"I'm sorry, what?" I take a step closer to this jackass. I know I don't have to try to look menacing. Just the way he's looking at Frankie has my blood boiling.

"Easy man. Just asking. She's hot. I'd like to tap that."

"Are you serious? She's our coach."

"Doesn't mean she's not hot."

If I don't leave this conversation now, I'm going to punch this guy. And that's not going to do me any good.

It finally felt like Frankie and I were on stable ground. I

know she's always had her worries about the age difference between the two of us, but after this last week?

Things have been good.

Now we have this dumbass to worry about.

*Why can't things ever be easy?*

"She's our coach. She's off-limits." I push past him, bumping into him with more force than necessary. I want to lay him out.

Maybe we won't be using tackling dummies and I can level him.

Frankie calls the first play and we line up. It's a play I've run hundreds of times. One I could easily run in my sleep.

My focus isn't on the play. It's on the guy who spins off the line faster than I do and gets to the target first.

"Great job, Lucas. You've got a good spin move." Frankie smiles at him after the play is over. "Maybe you can teach a few of our guys how you did that."

"You got it, Coach."

He winks at her.

She doesn't see it, but Lucas is looking at her like she's his next target.

When I came into practice today, this was the last thing I expected. It doesn't matter what Coach said. My position here doesn't feel safe. It feel like they're looking for my replacement.

Plus, if I'm gone? That means the end of this thing between me and Frankie.

Fuck.

Mondays are the worst.

# Chapter Twenty-Three

KNOX

"Did you hear the news?" Alex slaps me on the back as he takes the seat next to me.

"What news?"

"Kansas City's quarterback is out. Didn't clear concussion protocol."

I scrub a hand down my face. "Shit. Really?"

Alex nods. "Their backup has been practicing, but from what I've been told, he's having trouble."

A smile spreads across my face on its own. I couldn't help it if I tried. "Is it bad that makes me happy?"

"Nope. Should make our game easier tomorrow."

"It just made the division that much easier."

With Dallas beating Kansas City last week, it'll make winning the division even more likely for us. We needed some help after losing in London.

"Think you'll be ready?" Alex asks.

"Fuck off. Of course I will be."

My phone buzzes in my pocket. Pulling it out, I see my mom's name. Knowing she doesn't call me the night before a game, it sets a panic buzzing in my veins before I even pick up.

"I need to take this."

Alex nods as I walk out into the quiet hallway.

"Hey Mom."

"Hi, sweetheart."

The second my mom says hi, I know something's wrong. It's the Mom voice.

"What's wrong?"

"It's Grandma, sweetheart. She…died."

My knees give out as I sink to the wall behind me. "What?"

"I'm so sorry, Knox."

"I just talked to her this morning."

This can't be happening.

Mom's hiccups come through the phone. She's never been one to shy away from her emotions, but right now, it's too much.

"They said she complained of being tired after lunch and went to take a nap, and when she didn't come down for dinner, they sent someone to check on her."

"She's gone?"

"She's gone," Mom echoes.

Fat tears roll down my face unchecked. It feels like my heart is being ripped out of my chest.

"I'll be flying out there this week. There's a bit of logistics to take care of."

I nod along to my mom's words, not really hearing her.

My grandma has been there for me my entire life.

When my dad left, she was there.

When I needed someone to help me practice football after my grandpa died, she was there.

She's always been there.

Always.

And just like that, she's gone.

"Knox? Are you okay?" Coach Brooks's voice startles me.

"Honey, are you still there?"

"Listen, Mom, I need to go."

"Oh, okay. Call me later?"

I nod, even though I know she can't see me. "Love you."

"Love you." She hangs up and I stand, furiously wiping my tears away. "You need something, Coach?"

"What's going on?"

He gives me that look of his, the one that says he won't put up with anything less than the truth.

I blow out a breath. I don't want to say it out loud. Saying it means it's true. That she really isn't coming back.

"My, uhh…"

Coach steps closer, gripping my shoulders. It's about the only hold on reality I have right now. "Tell me what happened."

"My grandma died," I whisper.

He pulls me in for a hug, and the tears fall faster.

"I'm so sorry, son."

He lets me cry on his shoulder for who knows how long.

"What can I do for you? Do you need to head home tonight?"

"No," I snap, pulling back. "I need to be here."

"I don't know if that's a good idea." Coach crosses his arms, pinning me with another hard stare.

"I need this," I plead. "Otherwise, I'm going to be spinning my wheels all night."

"Tomorrow only." He points a finger in my face. "I don't want to see you next week at all."

"I understand."

I start to head toward the elevators, but Coach stops me.

"Knox."

"Yeah?" I shove my hands in my pockets.

"Don't push your feelings down. Lean on your people. Losing someone you love is never easy, and I don't want this to eat you up inside. Take the time you need. Football can wait."

I pound the button to the elevator. It's not coming fast enough. The last thing I want is to be out here and on display for everyone to see.

The doors finally open and I step inside, breathing a sigh of relief that the car is empty. I hesitate, not knowing which floor I should push.

Everything inside me is screaming to go see Frankie. To be in her arms as I unload every emotion I'm feeling right now.

Sadness.

Anger.

Rage.

The only person I want to see right now is her.

Except I don't. I press the button to my floor.

I don't know what stops me. Instead of going to Frankie, I go back to my room.

My empty room.

To drown my sorrows.

Because I lost one of the most important people in my life.

And I have no idea what to do with myself.

"KNOX. YOU MISSED ANOTHER BLOCK." The minute I'm off the field, Frankie is in my face.

"He's hard to stop."

Brown eyes look back at me in a challenge. "You're letting him get the drop on you."

"I know, Frankie."

"If you—"

"I said I know," I snap.

"Then if you know, why aren't you doing it?"

Her words are sharp as she walks down the rest of the line.

Fuck.

I ignore the stares of my teammates I feel on me as I sit on the bench. I thought I was doing a better job controlling my emotions, but I guess I'm not.

Alex and the offense are stopped on the next drive. I go to grab my helmet, but Frankie is holding a hand out. "We're sending in Black."

Oh, fuck no.

"You're kidding me."

"Knox, you haven't stopped them all day." She waves a hand in front of me. "Something is going on and your head is not in the game."

"Fuck that. I'll be fine."

"Then be fine on the bench."

Lucas runs past me, and I'm ready to charge after him and yank him back to the sideline, especially when he looks at me and calls out, "I'll show you how it's done."

Un-fucking-believable.

"Really? This guy? He's a dick."

"Right now, he's going to try and help us get this game under control." Her gaze is fierce. "Now, sit down, Knox." Frankie's hand stops me from doing what I want to do.

I glare down at her, unable to keep my anger in check. "You don't know what you're doing."

She stands taller, adjusting the hat on her head. "We need to stop Kansas City. The game is still within reach, and I need players out there whose heads are in the game." She takes a step back. "Don't make me tell you again."

I throw my helmet toward the bench, the plastic crashing into the metal. I'm sure every camera in the stadium has this on film, but right now, I don't care.

The exact thing Frankie said wouldn't happen is happening. I'm being replaced. By some two-bit chump who thinks he's God's gift to football.

I'm alone on the bench for the rest of the game. No one comes near me. It's like my bad energy radiates to the rest of the team. We lose a close game, one that we easily expected to win. I did nothing to help my team try to rally.

Some captain I am.

I take an extra long shower to avoid the post-game press. And the guys. I know I should tell them, but I'm not ready to face them and their words of sympathy.

By the time I'm changed, the locker room is blissfully empty.

Well, almost empty.

"What the hell was that, Knox?" I turn, and Frankie is there, ready to lay into me.

"You mean you benching me?"

She scoffs. "You couldn't block the broad side of a barn if you tried today. Whoever was out on that field, it wasn't you."

"I would've cleaned it up."

"I did what was best for the team," she hisses at me.

"And that's Lucas? He's an entitled asshole."

"It doesn't matter if he's an entitled asshole. His head was in the game today."

It's like I don't even know the person standing before me. Sure, she's Frankie, but the mask is up. I've always been able to read her like an open book.

Now? Nothing.

I don't know if it's because of her anger at me, or my own raging emotions, but in this moment, it hits me.

Frankie will always be my coach. She'll prioritize it over me every time. Whatever she feels for me is second to that.

The team first.

Knox second.

Message received.

My already cracked heart splits even more. I'm at the end of my limit.

"Then I'm doing what's best for me," I spit the words out. "We're done."

"What?" She rears back.

I wave a finger between the two of us. "You and me? We're over."

"Knox." She goes to touch me but pulls back. It confirms every suspicion I have.

"I guess you don't have to worry about getting fired anymore." I turn my back on her, grabbing my bag from my locker. "You say you're all in, but you've had one foot out of this relationship since we started."

"That's not true."

I shake my head. "You've been looking for a reason to end this."

"That's it? After everything we've been through?"

"Yup." I turn around. Her face is still rigid, not showing any emotion. I have no idea what my own face looks like. Pissed off. Sad. Hurt. "I'll see ya around, Frankie."

And just like that, it's over.

I leave the pieces of my heart on the floor with the woman who I wanted to give it to.

I guess I can't have everything. It was always going to be one or the other.

Frankie or football.

I guess I have my answer.

# Chapter Twenty-Four

"Newman! You're blocking low again. You need to aim higher!" I blow my whistle at him again, my frustration seeping out. It's like everything he learned before pulling his quad has left his brain.

"Sorry, Coach."

"Don't be sorry. Just block like I know you can."

"Hit 'em hard. Hit 'em clean." He nods and gets back into the practice lineup. The loss on Sunday was jarring to say the least. Everyone expected to win, even if we didn't say it. It's making practice that much harder this week.

With Knox gone, the morale of the defense has taken another hit. Guys have been asking me all week where he is, but no one from the team has told us anything.

*Personal reasons.*

Now that Knox and I are no longer…well, whatever we were, I have no right to know. Or ask.

And it's driving me crazy.

I try to push the thoughts from my head, but it's easier said than done. All week I've been thinking about him. Trying to figure out what changed.

The Knox in the locker room wasn't the one I've grown to love all these years. The one who loved his teammates more than anything. His family. Who sat and watched rom-coms with me and ate ice cream. Who held me as I cried after I was hit on the field.

That's the Knox I love. The one on Sunday pushed me away like I meant nothing to him, while also taking my heart with him.

I blink, turning my attention back to practice. It's what I need to be focusing on.

"Frankie. Why don't we try moving Newman over to the left side and see how he works there?" Coach Jenkins comes up beside me.

"Left?" That's where Knox lines up.

"Word just came down from Coach. He's out this week."

"Is he hurt?"

In all the years I've been coaching Knox, he's only missed a handful of games. All due to injury.

Coach Jenkins shakes his head. "You know as much as I do."

"Well, how long is he going to be out?" I shift the beanie on my head, nerves roiling through me.

"I don't know."

"Our captain is out and we don't know for how long. Is he gone for the rest of the season? How are we supposed to plan for the games when we have no idea if he'll be playing?"

"Look, Frankie,"—he gives his head an exasperated shake—"I don't know anything either and I don't like it. There's not much we can do unless someone tells us."

"But why aren't they telling us?"

He shrugs his shoulders and heads back over to the line.

Practice drags on. With Knox gone, it seems like no one has the heart to put into it. Even with a big divisional matchup coming up this weekend.

After another missed block, I blow my whistle. "Alright guys. Let's call it. Hit the weight room and we'll be done for the day."

Half of the guys head straight inside, not wanting to be called back out. The other half grab water and linger on the field.

"I promise I'll do better tomorrow, Coach." Newman looks dejected as he drops down on the field next to me.

"You're a great player. Great players all have off days. Rest up tonight and we'll get back at it tomorrow."

He gives me a grateful smile as Coach Brooks walks over to us.

"If you have a minute, can I talk to you in my office?"

"Me?" I point to myself, unsure which one of us he's talking to.

"Yes, you." He laughs. "Is that okay?"

I shake the paranoia from my head. "Sure."

"You look like you're going to puke," Newman says as I watch Coach's retreating form.

"Do you want to do laps?"

"Shit, no." He jumps up and heads inside.

I follow behind him at a much slower pace. There was nothing about Coach's tone that would tell me I'm in trouble.

But any time I'm called to his office, it feels like I'm in trouble. Like my secret has been exposed and I'll be fired on the spot.

My pace gets slower with each step closer to the office. The practice building's walls are lined with photos of past Mountain Lions. Of awards won.

*Will this be the last time I walk these halls?*

Getting to the coach's office, I take a steadying breath before knocking.

"Come in."

Pushing the door open, I step inside his office.

"You don't need to look so worried, Frankie." Coach Brooks looks relaxed, leaning back in his chair with a smile on his face.

"It feels like getting called to the principal's office."

"Well, this is hopefully better than that. Take a seat."

Sitting, I shove my hands under my legs to stop from fidgeting. "What'd you want to see me for?"

"Job is yours."

"I'm sorry, what?"

"You're officially the linebackers coach. Job is yours if you want it."

I'm stunned into silence.

For as long as I can remember, I've wanted to be a head coach. To work my way up and lead a team in all aspects to victory.

I started out as an assistant in the equipment department with the Mountain Lions. And now, here I am, more than a decade later and I'm finally getting the chance to lead part of the team.

It may not be the ultimate goal, but it's one step closer.

And sitting here today, in the coach's office, it somehow feels wrong.

"I really don't know what to say."

The smile slides off Coach's face. "I was hoping it would be an easy yes."

It would have been. Knox's face from Sunday fills my head. The dejected look on it. He ended things between us. There's no reason this job can't be mine.

*Just say yes.*

But I can't. Because of Knox.

"I can't."

"You can't? Frankie, this is a great opportunity for you. I know your goal is to be sitting here." He points to his own chair. "I thought this was what you wanted?"

"It was…"

"What changed?" Coach leans forward, steepling his fingers together. His eyes are studying.

I blow out a breath. Now is the time to come clean. To tell him everything. Because the only way I can have a future with this team is with a clear conscience.

*Or no future at all.*

"I have to tell you something and you're probably not going to like it."

"What is it?" His face gets hard.

"I've been sleeping with one of the players."

It's so quiet, you can hear a pin drop. Heat crawls up my cheeks as he stares at me.

*Oh God, he's going to fire me on the spot.*

"I'm sorry, what?"

"I—"

He holds up a hand. "I heard you. I can't believe it is all."

I want to look away, but it's hard to when it feels like he can see right through. I fight the urge to shift in my chair.

"And why are you telling me this now?"

"I love this team, Coach. I never wanted to do anything to jeopardize my position here. And even though what this player and I had ended, I couldn't take this promotion in good conscience. I respect you too much."

He scrubs a hand down his face. "You're one of the best damn coaches I've ever worked with, Frankie. That makes this really hard."

My lip quivers. "Am I fired?"

He shakes his head at me. "I don't know. I've never had

to worry about this before. Why even tell me? If you ended this like you say you did, why bother?"

I swallow around the rising lump of emotion in my throat. Every moment with Knox over the last few years plays back in my mind.

It was casual. We kept it only during the season. Neither of us wanted to risk our positions with the team if we were caught together during the offseason.

No matter how much I tried to deny it, I fell in love with Knox along the way. I've never wanted anyone the way I've wanted him.

"I love him. If denying it meant getting the promotion, I don't want it. There will be other jobs out there, but there's only one Knox."

I slap a hand over my mouth. Shit.

"Really? Our captain?"

"Would it have been better if it was a rookie?"

He groans again. "No."

I chew on my lip, trying to keep the emotions at bay.

"I don't know what I'm going to do here, Frankie. You've put me in a really tough spot."

I nod, for fear that I'll start crying if I speak.

"Come in tomorrow. I want practice to go off as normal. The guys are already having a hard enough time with Knox being gone for the next few weeks. I'll talk with management and see what they want to do."

That perks my attention up. "Do you know why he's gone?"

"You don't know?"

I shake my head.

"He didn't want me telling anyone, but his grandma passed away."

"Darlene died?" I gasp. "When?"

"Before the game last week."

My eyes shut on their own.

It all makes so much more sense now. His reaction to benching him was way out of line. He was lashing out because his grandma died.

My already broken heart crumbles. Knox loved his grandma more than anyone. I can't imagine what he's going through right now.

"Are you okay?" Coach asks. His face has softened, but he still doesn't look happy with me.

"Knox was acting out of character after the game. I guess I now know why."

"It's never easy losing someone we love." Coach stands and I follow. "We'll talk more tomorrow."

I turn to go but stop. "For what it's worth, I'm not sorry."

"You're not?"

I shake my head. "No. Am I sorry I'm putting you in this position? More than you'll ever know. I love him. Probably more than I realize and more than he realizes. And if there's even the chance that the two of us might have a future together, I want to take it. If I'm fired and I have to start over at the bottom, I will. Don't get me wrong, it'll suck, but Knox is worth it."

He's worth everything.

Coach nods. "I'll see you tomorrow, Frankie."

# Chapter Twenty-Five

## KNOX

"The one thing Darlene didn't have picked out was the urn. We have a few samples you can look at if you'd like to pick one out."

The funeral director is too made up, his face not showing an ounce of care. I don't know how my mom has the patience to deal with him, but she does. She's a saint. I would've snapped at him already.

"Knox?" A warm hand on my arm shifts my attention back to my mom. "Would you like to take a look at them with me?"

Her eyes are red-rimmed, like they have been all week.

"What does it matter? It's not like she'll care what she's in," I grumble.

"I'll give you two a minute." The man in front of us leaves the room, shutting the door quietly behind him.

"You don't have to be rude." I try to answer, but Mom just cuts me off. "And before you even think about saying you're not, I would advise you to think twice."

Fuck.

The last person I should be taking my anger out on is my mom. She's had just as rough of a week as I have.

Except she doesn't know the other reason I'm so bitter. The one that has nothing to do with my grandma and everything to do with the woman I walked away from in Denver.

"Sorry. There's just a lot going on, and I don't have the usual outlet of tackling dummies at practice to help."

"It still doesn't excuse your behavior." Leave it to my mother to put me in my place. "What's really going on?"

Mom pins me with a stare so fierce, it reminds me of my grandma. It has my already cracked heart splitting open that much more.

"There's someone back home, well, was someone back home. And now there's not."

"Ahh." Mom stands, reaching her hand out to me. "Let's go take a walk."

My eyebrows pull together in confusion. "Don't we need to finish making arrangements?"

"It'll keep."

Pushing open the door, I follow her out onto the wooded grounds. Stray leaves cling to the trees in an effort to hang on to the last of their lives. The grass is long since dead and the sky is a morose gray color.

Matching my mood perfectly.

"What happened?" Mom links her arm with mine as we stroll on the path through the burial grounds. Our feet carry us on a well-trod path that I know well. Grandma is being buried right next to my grandpa.

"We weren't allowed to be together." I kick a rock out of the way. "It's not like we had an actual future."

"Can I assume the woman in question is Frankie?"

I stop, not sure I'm hearing her correctly. "How the hell do you know that?"

"Honey, I'm not blind. Your grandma and I could both see it. Your grandma especially."

"She did?"

She nods, linking her arm through mine as we walk a familiar path to where my grandpa is buried. "After you and Frankie played games with her, she called me and told me you met your match."

"Why didn't she tell me?"

Mom laughs, a deep happy sound that I haven't heard in a few days. "For being raised by two women, you sure don't clue in to a lot of things."

"Oh yeah?" I cross my arms. "Like what?"

"Grandma could see how much she cared for you when she came to the retirement center. She saw it again when we were in London."

I drop down onto a nearby bench. "I thought she was being polite by inviting her out."

Mom sits next to me. "Polite, yes. But you can politely say no too. She wanted to be with you just as much as you did."

"Fuck."

"Language." Mom smacks me on the arm. "For the first time in a long time, you looked happy."

"I've always been happy."

"You enjoy football, yes. But you needed something outside of the game. And she gave you that. We were both always so worried that you wouldn't find anyone because of the way your father left, and neither one of us wanted you to spend your life alone."

I hate that even all these years later, my dad leaving is still a wound that I can't get past. No matter how hard I've tried, it's always lingering. And it caused me to push away the best thing that's ever happened to me—all because I was scared she was replacing me with someone else.

"I don't deserve her."

"I don't believe that for a second."

I kick my legs out in front of me, letting the cold air seep into my bones. Maybe it'll make this hurt less. The ache has been constant. One minute I'm missing Grandma, and the next, Frankie. It's never-ending.

"I freaked out on her. She pulled me from the game and I lost it."

"A game which you shouldn't have been playing in the first place," Mom points out.

I huff out a laugh, the first one in a week. "I know."

"If your grandma were here, she'd say you were being pigheaded."

A watery smile spreads across my face. "I'm sure she'd have a few other choice words to add."

"She would. But what you did to Frankie, is it something you can apologize for?"

I scrub a hand down my face. "Sure. But it doesn't change the reality of our situation."

Mom crosses her arms and turns to face me. "Do you love her?"

"Of course I do." My tone is more defensive than I mean it to be.

"So change your situation." She states it like it's the easiest thing to do.

"She's my coach, Mom. Not really something I can change unless one of us changes teams. And then what's the point?"

"Sweetheart, I love you, but sometimes you're rather dense." Mom laughs, wrapping an arm around my shoulders.

"Gee, thanks."

"If you love this woman like you say you do, you shouldn't let anything get in your way. One of the last conversations I had with Grandma was that she was happy knowing you'd be taken care of. That you'd found someone to put you in your place and keep you on your toes."

My eyes get wet at hearing that. Because it's the exact kind of thing she would like.

"Frankie reminds me of her. She's strong. Never letting me get away with anything, but always making me feel like I could do anything I put my mind to."

"You need someone like that. Don't let her go just because of your circumstances. If she's as strong as you say she is, you're going to need to fight for her."

A weight lifts off my shoulders as I lean farther into my mom. "Hopefully she'll still be around to fight for when I get home."

"I don't doubt that for a second. Now, will you come help me pick out an urn so we can get out of here? This guy gives me the creeps."

Laughter bubbles out of me. "Only if it's a really ugly one."

Mom drops a kiss on my head and stands. "No one could ever deny you that you're hers. Let's do it."

# Chapter Twenty-Six

FRANKIE

"**F**rankie. Coach wants to talk to you," one of the assistants yells at me from the sideline.

"Thanks. I'll be there as soon as we're done with reps."

"He said now."

Shit.

My stomach has been in my throat for days. I've been preparing like this will be my last week coaching. If I'm let go, no one is going to want to pick me up. I might be a great coach, but that doesn't mean another team would want the headache of picking me up.

It's not like I slept around.

I just happened to fall for the completely wrong guy.

"Alright, guys. Wind sprints. Ten laps and then call it." I nod to the assistant next to me and head toward the offices in the practice facility.

These walls have been my home away from home. I've poured everything I have into this team. I love this game more than anything and am not ready to part with it. With each step, I feel like I'm walking toward my own execution.

With a knock on the door, I'm called into Coach's office.

"You wanted to see me?"

"Take a seat, Frankie." Coach drops his glasses next to his computer as I sit in front of his desk. I can see my guys through the window on the practice field. His face is tight, unflinching. I don't know the last time I've seen him without a smile. This stern look makes me queasy. He's always been one of the most easygoing people.

I hate that I'm the one on the receiving end of this.

"You've put me in a really tough position, Frankie."

"I know. And I'm sorry." I sit on my hands, trying to do anything to stop the nerves from exploding out of me. "I didn't mean for this to happen."

"It's not something I've ever had to worry about before. My coaches falling for players."

I snort. "Believe me, it's not something I wanted to happen. It just sort of did."

"This entire situation is unprecedented. There's a no-fraternization policy between coaches and players, but this is the first time it's ever come up."

"Because I'm one of the only female coaches in the league," I sigh.

"One of two now, to be exact."

"What does it mean for me?"

"We can't promote you to linebackers coach. I'm sorry, Frankie, but it would be too messy."

My heart drops. All I've ever wanted, ever since my brother started playing football in the backyard, was to be a coach.

And I've completely ruined my chance.

"I understand."

"Coach Reich is going to take over the linebackers and we're shifting you to safeties coach."

"You are?" I can't hide the shock in my voice.

"I'm going to be straight with you, Frankie." Coach stands and walks around the desk. "You're a good coach—"

"For a woman?" I hate that there's always that caveat stuck on the end.

"No. Period. You're one of the best I've worked with. You don't take shit from the guys, and you're always finding new ways to better the entire line. It's why we don't want to let you go. Even though you broke the rules, management doesn't want to lose you to another team."

"Really?" My voice is soft. Being one of the only women coaching in this league has made it hard. I've had to fight for every inch I've gained. Even then, they'd be small victories, and I'd have to keep fighting for the next.

"Really. But we have some ground rules."

"Anything."

"No interfering. You don't like the decision they make regarding linebackers? Keep it to yourself. You have one shot at this. If you show any kind of favoritism toward Knox by using your position, you're gone."

I swallow. "Understood."

"I mean it. I don't want to have to deal with guys crying to me because the coaches made a decision so your boyfriend wouldn't be sad."

I laugh at that. "I don't think anyone could accuse me of favoritism when I benched him on Sunday."

Coach points at me. "But it showed you can make the hard choices when necessary. It's hard doing that when you're a coach. And that's why I fought for you. It couldn't have been easy."

I wince, still hating I had to make that decision. "It was for the good of the team."

He nods. "And while I don't think Knox would've agreed at the time, you put the team first."

"I love this team, Coach. And I'm sorry if my actions put the team in jeopardy. I'll do whatever it takes to show you that and get back into your good graces."

"Just do the job I know you can do. Our safeties need the work, and if there's anyone who can turn them around, it's you."

"You got it." I breathe a sigh of relief. The promotion I dreamed of getting may be gone, but I'm lucky to still have a job.

"Management is suspending you one week, with pay, as punishment."

"With pay?"

"With pay. I recommend taking the time to relearn the playbook with our safeties in mind."

I try to fight the smile on my face. "And my relationship?"

"That's for you to work out with Knox. But HR will have some forms for you to fill out should you decide to continue your relationship."

Coach moves around the desk and takes his seat, effectively dismissing me.

I stand. "Thank you, Coach. I know you could've fired me and been done with it, but thank you for going to bat for me."

He gives me a soft smile. "You've got what it takes to go far, Frankie. Hopefully this is just a bump in the road on your way to becoming a head coach."

I suck in a breath. Yes, this has always been my dream. But this is the first time someone other than me has acknowledged it.

"Now get out of here."

"Can I ask a favor before I go?" I squeeze my hands in front of me.

Our relationship is out in the open. Or what's left of it. I don't know if there's a chance to salvage what we had, but I have to try.

Maybe now I can have the best of both worlds.

"Depends on what it is." Coach drops the pen in his hand.

"I know I'm suspended, but mind if I take a few of the guys with me? I want to be there for Knox, and I know they would want to be there too."

"Send them back to me before the game in one piece."

# Chapter Twenty-Seven

FRANKIE

Suspended.

Holy shit. That could have gone so much worse, but it didn't.

Suspended. With pay.

Sure, I might've blown up my promotion, but I still have a job. It might take me awhile to get a promotion or move up, but I'll put in the work.

My hands are shaking as I head into the weight room, hoping to find the guys. Except when I turn the corner, I run smack into Colin.

"Frankie. Hi."

I blow out a breath. "Hi."

"You okay?"

"Actually, I need to talk to you."

"Me?" He points at himself. "Why?"

"Well, you, Jackson, Logan, and Alex."

"Again, why? What could you possibly need with the four of us?"

Maybe it wasn't good luck running into him. This would've been easier with Alex.

"It's about Knox. Do you talk to all of your coaches this way?"

He shifts, looking me over as if wondering if he can trust me. "Follow me."

I walk after him, deeper and deeper into the building. Pushing open a door, I follow him into a small film room with the guys in question.

"What are you all doing here?" My eyes flit between all of them.

"You said you wanted to talk about Knox. That's what we were doing."

Alex stands up and crosses the room. His presence is powerful. It's always been like this. He's more than just the captain and the quarterback. He leads everyone in a way that is soft and commanding at the same time. People don't want to disappoint him because he lays it all out there for them, and he expects the same.

"Did Coach tell you what happened?" I eye each one of them.

Football players don't intimidate me. Never have. I've grown up around them, coached them for the last decade. I can put up with their egos.

But being around this group of guys has butterflies gathering in my stomach. I know how close Knox is with these guys. I'm already the outsider here.

"He did. Did he clue you in?" Colin asks, standing next to Alex. These guys are definitely the first line of defense in getting to Knox.

Spoiler alert. I already know.

"Yes. Seeing how I now have some time on my hands, I'm going to the funeral."

"But why? You two hate each other." Logan comes up on the other side of Alex while Jackson assesses the situation from where he's sitting.

"Like *hate* hate each other," Colin agrees. "You're always riding him about something he did wrong in practice or making him do extra weights. Why would you be going to the funeral if you hate each other?"

Men. Absolutely clueless.

"Knox and I don't hate each other—"

Colin snorts, interrupting me.

"Would you let her talk?" Alex whispers to him.

"It's not like they're…" Logan turns to me now, his eyes wide in shock. "Oh shit. You two are totally sleeping together!"

"No way."

"Are you fucking serious? No."

"Uh-uh. No way. Not happening."

"How long has this been going on?"

All of them are now shouting over each other. I let them, moving to sit next to Jackson, who is still just staring at me.

"You have anything to add to this?" I throw a thumb behind me. The three of them are now arguing with each other.

"Are you two happy?"

"I mean, we were."

"Were?" He leans forward. "Guys. Would you quit your arguing?" He looks exasperated, but they quiet down immediately.

Shifting, I face the guys, then Jackson. "You'll need to show me how you do that. Sometimes I can't get the guys to listen that well at practice."

"Only works on people who act like five-year-olds." He smirks.

"Hey. I am more mature than these two," Alex whines.

"I…"—Colin thinks about it—"no, you're right. You

are. But how can anyone expect us to keep our cool when you tell us you two have been sleeping together?"

"I figured it out," Logan pipes up.

"You guessed," I correct.

"Same thing. I still figured it out before these guys."

"Then I'll buy you a cookie," Colin tells him. "What I want to know is details."

I cringe. "You don't need details."

Colin waves me off. "I don't want gross details. God, Frankie. Head out of the gutter. Jesus, you'd think you coach football players or something."

"Good. Because you weren't getting any."

"Okay, this is kind of freaking me out." Logan takes a seat across the table from me. "Now that I know this, I feel like you and Knox are so similar, it makes so much sense."

"Stop trying to act like you knew," Jackson tells him. "But really. How long?"

I stare at the ceiling, trying to think how long it's been since that fateful storm in Buffalo.

"About four years? Give or take."

That shuts them all up. Jaws are on the floor as they all look at me, clearly trying to piece together how they never realized it.

"Four years? You and Knox have been together that long?" Alex asks.

"Technically less. We were only together during the season so no one would find out."

"I don't understand how you did it." Alex is in awe. "I could barely handle a few months sneaking around with Carter before I cracked."

"Wait." Jackson holds out a hand. "All those times you came looking for him to go over film?"

I scrunch my face up, nodding at him. He makes it sound so scandalous.

"Holy shit. I thought he was just the worst player."

"Knox is one of the best players I've ever coached. And that includes Roberts." Roberts who just went into the Hall of Fame this past summer.

"Wow. All these years. I kind of feel like an idiot for not noticing," Alex states. "Why tell us now?"

"Let's just say things got a bit more complicated."

"You mean Knox lost his shit and left town and didn't tell anyone about his grandma until we all badgered the shit out of him?" Logan says bluntly.

"Well, yes."

"What do you plan to do with Knox?" Colin crosses his arms and leans against the table. Sensing he's trying to be imposing, all it does is make me laugh.

"I'm sorry, but are you trying to shake me down?"

He looks around at the other guys before looking affronted. "No. I'm just looking out for him."

"He's asking what your intentions are with our Knox." Alex flips his gaze from Colin to me. "We love Knox and if you two were just fooling around—"

"I'm sorry." I jump out of my seat. "Do you think I would blow up my career for anything less than love?"

"Did you get fired?" Jackson asks.

I shake my head. "No. But instead of getting promoted, I'm being shifted to safeties."

"And you did all of this for Knox?" Alex pipes in.

I blow out a breath, frustration starting to creep in. "Yes. What do you need me to tell you in order for you to believe my feelings for Knox?"

"It's hard to shift gears," Colin says. "For years, Knox has been complaining about you, but now we find out you two have been...well, that." He cringes at the thought.

"Oh, grow up, Colin," Logan jests. "I for one am

happy if Knox is happy." The look he gives me says I better know the answer there.

"I wish I knew the answer to that. Knox and I had a huge fight after the game and now I don't know where things stand."

"You blew up your career, and you don't know where you stand with Knox?" Colin questions.

I nod. "Yes."

"Shit. You really do love him."

I roll my eyes. "I'm glad that confirms what I've been telling you."

"What are you going to do about it?" Alex asks. "We've all been there, screwed up. Are you planning on fixing it?"

I look at each of them. Guys I know through the team, but not well. Sitting here with them now, I see why Knox loves them so much.

"Considering I have some time on my hands, I plan on going out to the funeral. I don't know if he'll want to see me or not, but I'm going to try. He shouldn't be alone right now."

Alex waves around them. "We were also planning on going. Coach said the owner can loan us his jet so we can get there and back before the game this weekend."

"Mind if I tag along then?"

"As long as you don't plan on breaking his heart."

"Trust me, all of you, if anyone's heart is going to break, it's mine. Because I love him and I don't know if he'll take me back."

They all exchange a glance.

"Oh, that big lovable, goofball will take you back. Trust us."

God, I hope they're right. Because I do love that big goofball.

And I want him back more than anything.

# Chapter Twenty-Eight

KNOX

"Stop fidgeting." My mom swats my hands away from my tie.

"Sorry." Stuffing my hands into my pockets, I rock back onto my heels as the last few guests file into the funeral home. "I hate suits."

"You wear them every week for games," she points out.

"Yes, but it doesn't mean I like them."

"It's only because he doesn't look as good as I do wearing one."

I whip around at the sound of Colin's voice. Alex, Logan, and Jackson are all with him. "What the fuck are you guys doing here?"

Another swat from Mom. "Language."

"What are you guys doing here?" I correct myself.

Mom squeezes my arm. "I'll give you a few minutes. I'll come get you before we start."

"Thanks." I give her a grateful smile. "We have a game on Sunday."

Colin rolls his eyes at me. "We got the private jet. We're fine."

"How are you doing?" Alex asks, stepping inside.

I shrug a shoulder. "I've been better. It's good to see you guys, though."

Colin wraps an arm around my shoulders, pulling me in for a hug. It's then that I see Frankie standing behind them.

Fuck, is she ever a sight for sore eyes.

"I'm really sorry, Knox. Darlene was an incredible person and I know I'll miss her."

Colin's words have me choking up. "She was."

"I wish I got to know her better," Logan says.

Colin steps back as Logan hugs me. "She liked you. All of you guys."

My gaze keeps flitting to Frankie. I want to pull her into my arms and unleash all the pent-up emotions I've been feeling this week.

"I can't believe all of you guys came out here."

Jackson shakes his head, stepping in to hug me. "Of course we'd be here. We're family."

I squeeze him a little tighter. "Thanks, man. Really." My voice cracks.

Alex peers over his shoulder. "We'll give you a minute."

Alex and Jackson slap me on the shoulder as they head inside.

"But don't think we're not going to discuss this," Colin says, pointing a finger in my face.

A smirk pulls at my mouth. "Okay."

"Seriously," Logan backs him up. "How did we not know about this?"

I push him in after Colin. "Because we didn't tell anyone."

"I'd yell at you, but I'm afraid your mom would yell at me."

"You're not wrong," I agree with a chuckle.

He shakes his head as I take a step toward Frankie. We're the only two left in the welcoming area.

"Hi."

God, I've missed the sound of her voice.

"Hi. How are you?"

"I'm sorry about your grandma."

We're talking over each other. Frankie tucks a stray lock of hair behind her ear. She looks formal—too formal—in a black dress with her hair pulled up on top of her head in a fancy bun. So unlike the Frankie I'm used to seeing every day.

The silence stretches between us. It's a new feeling, and not a welcome one. Frankie's eyes don't stray from mine. She's the first to break the silence.

"Why didn't you tell me your grandma died?"

"Because if I told you, it would've been real. And I wasn't ready to accept it."

Frankie takes a step closer to me, her hands reaching out to smooth the lapels of my jacket. "You didn't have to go through it alone."

I cover her hand with mine, warmth radiating out from her. "I…"

I'm at a loss for words. All my life, I only relied on those that I knew wouldn't leave.

Mom.

Grandpa.

Grandma.

Everyone else left me. I never wanted to be vulnerable with them because I didn't want to show them I needed them.

It was one big lie.

Because I do need people. And as much as I told myself I didn't have anyone I could rely on, I did.

The guys.

Coach.

Frankie.

Instead of pushing her away, I should've held on tight.

I only hope I haven't blown it.

She cups my cheek. I lean into her touch, savoring it and feeling at peace for the first time since I got the news. "Knox—"

"Sweetheart, we're getting ready to start," Mom interrupts.

Frankie starts to step back, but I pull her back in. "Will you sit with me?"

Reaching out, Frankie takes my hand in hers. "There is nowhere else I would rather be."

Frankie

THE SERVICE GOES by in the blink of an eye. Knox held on to me the entire time. His tears brought out my own. And after, the guys and I went to Shannon's house to set up the reception while she and Knox attended a private burial.

"Frankie, you don't need to be doing the dishes," Shannon barks out at me after the reception as the last dish is set next to the sink.

"It's the last thing you need to be worried about right now."

"It's a good distraction."

"I don't mind helping. I can stay and help if you need anything else?" I hang the dirty dish towel over the sink.

She walks over, wrapping me in a hug. "I'm fine. I

think someone else could use you more." She pulls back, smoothing her hands over my hair. "Thank you for coming. Thank you for being here for Knox. Whether he tells you or not, he needs you more than you know."

Tears prick my eyes. "I just hope I'm not too late."

"Oh dear." She pulls me in for a hug. "Sometimes Knox doesn't know how to handle his feelings, but I know love when I see it. And you two have it in spades."

A stray tear slips through. "Thank you."

"Now, go find him. I'll take care of putting away the leftovers." Shannon shoos me out of the kitchen. Grabbing a beer, I follow the sounds of laughter outside.

A fire crackles in the bonfire pit. Knox and the guys are standing around, beers in hand.

"She's the reason we couldn't play bingo anymore. Who gets into a fight playing bingo?" Colin's voice is exasperated. "I swear, playing football is easier than playing bingo with Darlene!"

Knox laughs, a real laugh. It's a sound I've missed. It took him leaving for me to see what I actually want in life.

"And then dominoes got banned too," Logan states, pointing a beer bottle in my direction. "Jackson almost got into a fistfight over it!"

He throws his hands up in defense, as I move into the group. "The only reason I didn't was because I forfeited. Do you know how hard that was?"

Knox winks at me as I move to stand next to him. Our arms brush, the sensation sending butterflies fluttering in my belly.

"You'd think they were playing for a million bucks,"— Alex shakes his head, sipping his beer—"not for candy bars."

"You think that'll be us when we're that age?" Jackson asks.

"Fuck, we'll be ten times worse!" Colin confirms. "None of us will ever quit!"

"I hate to break up this party, but we need to head to the airport." Alex sets his bottle down on the edge of the fire pit.

Everyone hugs Knox before heading inside.

"Take care of him, okay?" Logan says, giving me a hug as he passes.

"I will."

"He's lucky to have you."

I squeeze him a little tighter. "I'm lucky to have him too."

Even spending the last few hours with the guys, I know why Knox loves them so much. Denver only has good guys, but I haven't had the chance to get to know them.

I'm hoping that they'll be a part of my life going forward—because of the man standing in front of me.

"Don't you need to go with them?" Knox asks.

I shake my head. "I've been suspended for a week."

"What?" His voice booms around the quiet.

I hold up my hands, moving closer to him. "Suspended with pay. It could've been worse."

"What happened?" Knox rubs his eyebrow. "Fill me in."

I rehash everything that's happened in the last few days.

"But you didn't get fired?"

"No. I don't know if I'll ever get promoted, but that's okay."

"Frankie, no—"

I hold up a hand, cutting him off. "It's okay. A position will come. Maybe with Denver. Maybe not. But I realize what's most important."

"And what's that?"

The dying light of the fire illuminates his handsome face. "You. Us. Building a life together…if you'll have me."

Wrapping a hand around my waist, Knox pulls me into him. "Frankie, I screwed up. When my grandma died, I didn't handle it well. And I took it out on you."

I shake my head, but Knox keeps going.

"No. I should've told you, but I didn't. Because no one has ever stuck around for me. When you benched me and put in Black, I thought you were choosing him over me and I lost it."

Grabbing him by the lapels, I pull him to me. "You better hear this, Knox Fisher. I might've had my priorities out of whack, but I don't anymore. I want you. I love you, Knox, and I'm sorry if I ever made you feel otherwise."

"But you're okay with no promotion? I don't want to hide this anymore. I can't keep doing it."

"Understand this,"—grabbing the back of his neck, I pull him closer to me—"we can be together. I'm being transferred to the safeties, and I can't interfere with you and your coaching, but the plan is in place."

Knox hoists me into his arms. "I'm sorry, Frankie. I know how much you wanted that promotion."

I nod. "It hurts, but it would hurt even more to lose you."

"You won't keep looking for a reason to end this? I know you hate how much older you are…" His voice trails off.

I smile back at him. "I'm all in, with both feet."

A smug grin lights up his face. "You love me?"

I drag a hand through his hair. Being in his arms like this is something I didn't think I'd get to have again. "So damn much that I can't keep lying to myself about this."

Knox closes the distance between our mouths, a fiery

kiss lighting every nerve of my body, something only Knox can make me feel. His tongue tangles with mine as we take each other in.

"I love you, Frankie. It might have taken a few years to get here, but I'm all in. You. Me. I want it all."

"Hell yes." I go back in for another kiss. I'm addicted. I never want to be without his kisses.

The air is cool around us as he finally pulls back.

"Stay with me tonight?" he whispers against my lips.

"You'd have to fight me to get me to leave."

Knox carries me into the now dark house. He doesn't stop until we're in his dimly lit room.

Our movements are unhurried as we reseal our connection. One that won't be broken by football or positions.

The two of us are in this.

Forever.

That's all we need to know as we come together, the love we feel for each other making our release even more intense.

I don't know how I thought I could ever deny myself of this man.

Because Knox is it.

Knox is everything.

Nothing else matters but the two of us.

Exactly how it should be.

# Chapter Twenty-Nine

KNOX

"Is it weird to be watching the game from the couch instead of playing?" Mom asks as the team runs out onto the field.

It's been a couple of days since the funeral. Thankfully, the team gave me the time off I needed. I wasn't in the right headspace after everything happened, so I'm grateful for the weeks of rest.

"I always watch from the sideline. Oh, were you talking to Knox?" Frankie laughs and pops a chip into her mouth.

"You're the one calling the plays," I tell her.

"Someone has to make you look good."

"I don't know why I put up with you." Wrapping an arm around her shoulders, I pull her closer to me in a tight, playful hold.

Her efforts to push me off of her are fruitless as I hold on tighter.

"It's because you love me."

"Eh, maybe." I let go, her face happy with laughter.

God, to think I almost pushed her away because I

couldn't have both sides of her. This woman is the best thing to ever happen to me.

"Are you two going to be okay if I leave you alone for a few hours?" Mom asks as the guys walk toward midfield for the coin toss.

"Sure thing, Mom." She drops a kiss on my forehead as she grabs her purse and walks outside.

"She didn't have to leave." Frankie burrows in even closer to me as the Mountain Lions kick off to start the game. "I know you two don't get to see each other much during the season."

"It's been a long two weeks for her. I think she wants some alone time."

"You're lucky to have such a great mom."

I smile down at Frankie. "She's the best. She more than made up for my dad leaving."

"I should be thankful for her and your grandparents. You turned out pretty great."

Leaning down, I take her lips in a sweet kiss, showing her how much I love her. Not many people would be willing to give up their careers, especially someone so passionate and driven as Frankie. But she did.

For me.

I don't know if I'll ever be worthy of her, but I'm going to fight every damn day to prove to her it wasn't in vain.

"Great sack for Black!" the announcer yells, breaking us apart.

Our attention turns back to the game. "Am I allowed to say he was a good pickup?" Frankie's voice is wary.

"You can say that. I'm not going to freak out on you. Even if he is a dick." I brush my fingers over her cheek, her eyes staring back at me with so much love. "You and all your wisdom from being *so much older* has taught me a thing or two."

"Only one or two?" She quirks a brow in my direction. "Damn. I'll need to work harder. He's a good player, but no one is ever going to replace you."

The fact that she can joke about this now calms me in a way I never thought I'd need. She's all in. I don't have to question it.

I sink farther into the couch, turning my focus back onto the game. The offense has now taken the field. "I know that now."

"Newman will be back soon and then it'll be the two of you on the line again."

"Do you regret giving up the promotion?" It's the one thought that's been plaguing me.

Frankie sits up, clasping my neck in her hands. My eyes don't leave hers. They're fiery, so I know she means business.

"I will never regret giving up that promotion for you. Never. I get to have the person I love most in the world and the game I love."

"If you're sure…"

"The only way I'd regret it is if I had to move to offense." She mock shudders.

"Yes, because working with Alex, Logan, and Colin would be so hard." I roll my eyes at her.

"Defense has always been my favorite. It's not just throwing yourself onto bodies to stop them. There's a method to the madness that most people don't realize, and I love it."

"Alex would make your job a lot easier." I point to the TV as Colin races into the end zone for an easy touchdown.

"Defense wins championships," she counters.

"Okay, fine. You win."

"Thank you." Frankie drops a peck on my lips and

goes back to watching the game. Colin is celebrating in the end zone.

"There's something else I wanted to talk to you about." It's been sitting in the back of my mind since I talked to my mom at the funeral home. Something I hope she's on board for.

"Oh yeah?" She doesn't look at me.

"Considering how long we've been together, some might ask what the next logical step in our relationship would be."

"Are you asking for you, or because people have actually been asking?"

"My mom gave me my grandma's rings when she died. She said she would've wanted me to have them to give to the woman I loved."

"Wait." This gets Frankie's attention as she moves onto my lap. "Did your grandma know?"

I laugh. "As she told my mom, a complete stranger could see how much we loved each other."

"And yet, no one on the team found out."

"I guess we were pretty good at hiding when we needed to." I wrap my arms around her waist and draw her in closer. "And let's face it, the guys are pretty clueless because they're all loved up."

"What's your question you're asking, Knox?" Frankie finds the necklace I always wear and starts fiddling with it, her nervous habit.

"I'm not proposing marriage yet, but is that something you'd want?"

Frankie blows out a breath, not looking at me.

"Is that something you want?" I tilt her chin up to look at me.

I'm waiting on pins and needles. I never really thought about marriage before now. With Frankie? I want her to be my forever. The person I'm with until I take my last breath. Because I love her more than anything on this entire planet.

Even more than football.

"I do, but if we get married now, won't people think I only have my job because of you?"

"No one would think that."

Frankie shakes her head at me. "Of course they would. I've worked hard to get where I am, and I don't want anyone to think I only got my position because of you."

"What has to happen then for me to propose? I retire? Because that isn't happening for years, Frankie."

"You've got too many good years left in you to wait around for that." She scrunches her face up in thought. "How about after a Super Bowl?"

"A win or loss?" I ask.

"Would you really want to propose if we lost?"

"It'd make the night better."

"But it'd make a win even more memorable," she points out.

"So I can't propose until we win a Super Bowl then?"

Frankie smiles down at me. "Maybe that'll add some extra motivation for you to get there."

I flip her over so her back is on the couch, my weight settling on top of her.

"Fine," I grumble. "A Super Bowl win. But you better be prepared, Rose, because the second we win, I'll be down on one knee. Can I settle for having you move in with me until then?"

"If that is your definition of settling, I think I'll be able to handle that."

We seal it with a kiss.

Oh yeah, I'm good with settling.

# Chapter Thirty



"Are you sure you want to do this?" Knox asks me again.

We flew home to Denver yesterday, and it's our first day back at practice. The morning was spent filling out forms with the team to ensure there wouldn't be any blowback on them. Now, we're heading out onto the practice field.

Me with the safeties, Knox with the linebackers.

It's going to be weird, but I'm ready.

"They're going to find out when they realize I'm not with you guys."

"They'll be jealous you're working with the safeties."

"Denver will have the best damn safeties in the league when I'm done with them." I beam up at him.

"Aww, look. It's the happy couple." Logan comes out of the locker room with Alex and Colin on his heels.

"Gross. Are we going to have to see you two necking all the time?" Colin asks.

"Necking? What are you, ninety?" Knox shoves him as he walks up to us.

"Like you have room to talk, Colin. You're in Peyton's office any chance you can get," Alex states.

"At least we keep it in her office." He waggles his eyebrows at Alex.

"Trust me, there'll be none of that between the two of us," I say, defiance in my voice.

"What, seriously?" Knox whips around to face me.

"Is this really a conversation you want to be having in front of the guys?"

"I'd abort if I were you." Jackson pats Knox on the shoulder as he heads out to the field. "I don't think it's going to end well for you."

"I feel like we should leave, but this is too good." Logan is grinning next to Colin.

"She's already got him by the balls. I love it." Colin leans against the wall.

"Alright, leave, you fuckers." Knox shoves them all down the hallway leading out to the field.

I've gotten to know these guys better over the last few weeks. They really are like brothers. Brothers who are way too involved in everyone else's business, but I love how much they care for each other.

"Did you really mean that?" Knox whispers as I take off after them. "I was kind of looking forward to a little hanky-panky in your office."

"Hanky-panky? Really, Knox?" I laugh at him. "For the first time, we don't have to hide our relationship. I plan on going home with you, and we can have all the hanky-panky you want in our bed."

Knox stops me, pulling me back into him. "I like the sound of that."

"Hanky-panky?" I tilt my lips up just a hair. His warm breath ghosts over them, ratcheting up my desire for him.

"No. Our bed." He drops a quick peck onto my lips and then bolts past me.

"That was just mean," I yell after him.

"I can say the same to you." He winks as he runs to where the linebackers are all waiting.

The skies are gray, and breaths are hanging above the field as the guys run drills. It's cold, with the game temperatures projected to be even colder. With snow forecasted on Sunday, we're practicing outside.

"Hey Coach! It's great to have you back!" Newman stops by the tackling dummies as I tug my hat down my head. "Hopefully we did you proud this week."

Now that the moment is here, nerves are getting the best of me.

"You always do, Newman." I smile at the rookie. He's one of the reasons I love coaching so much. Watching how far he's come this season is why I love what I do.

"What's on the agenda for practice today?" he asks, gripping his helmet in hand.

*Here goes nothing.*

"You're going to need to ask Coach Reich for that."

"What? Why?" He looks confused as the rest of the linebackers come up behind him. Knox goes to stand by him, giving me the nod to keep going.

"I'm moving over to safeties."

"But why? You're the best coach we've got."

Coach Jenkins and Reich choose that moment to come over. Coach Brooks filled them in, and while they were shocked at first, they've been supportive. Especially since they each got their own promotions. "What have I been doing then this whole season?"

"Sorry, Coach. It's just, well, Frankie has been working with me all season. She's the reason I've come so far."

Jenkins smiles back at him. "Don't you think it'd be fair then to let our safeties have her?"

"Don't get me wrong, Newman, I love working with you guys, but if I want to be with Knox here, I need to change lines."

There. I ripped the Band-Aid off. I watch as it dawns on them what I said. Knox is standing there with a bemused grin on his face.

"Wait, what?" Newman looks at Knox and then back at me, before shifting his gaze back to Knox. "You two are together?"

"And here I thought you were smarter than that," Knox says, punching him in the shoulder pads.

"Like, together together?" Newman asks again.

"I think we've blown his mind," Knox says, looking me dead in the eye.

"I think we did," I say with a laugh.

"Great, thanks for breaking my players when I take over." Coach Reich rolls his eyes at me. "Newman, you think you're going to be okay?"

"It's just…Coach Rose is always so hard on Knox."

"You think I was taking it easy on you?" I quirk a brow in his direction. "Because I can have Coach Reich here step it up if you think I'm not working you hard enough."

"Oh shit," he mumbles.

"I think just for that, everyone give me suicide drills." Coach Reich blows his whistle.

"Really, Newman? Really?" Knox groans. "You couldn't keep your mouth shut?"

"How am I supposed to when I find out you two are together? I have so many questions."

"If you don't quit asking, you're going to get us into even more trouble."

I can't help but laugh at the two of them as the rest of the linebackers join them.

"You're sure about this decision?" Coach asks.

I watch Knox's retreating form as he heads out to start running drills with the defense.

"Never been more sure of anything in my entire life."

KNOX - FOUR YEARS LATER

"Alright boys. One more stop and you know what happens," the defensive coordinator shouts. He can barely be heard over the noise in the stadium.

It's fourth and three, with less than two minutes to play. Houston's offense has the ball, but even if they make this play, they used their last time-out and are down by ten.

In the AFC Championship game.

My eyes find Frankie's across the huddle, and she sends a wink my way. There's no way we're not making this stop. Not only for me, but for the woman standing across from me. The energy in this group of guys is a live wire.

"You heard coach. Let's finish this game right now," I bellow to the group. It sends chills racing through me as they yell around me. The game every football professional, player and coach alike, works toward is within arm's reach.

I want this. Not only for me, but for every one of the guys standing around this huddle. They've busted their asses the last few years. To get so close and not make it is something that sticks with you.

And now, to be a part of this epic run we've had this year? With Frankie still at my side?

It's special.

Houston runs back onto the field.

I grab my helmet and tug it over my head.

"Bring it home, kid." Frankie is beaming at me under her beanie. It started snowing halfway through the game. Nothing to cause issues, but it's worked in our favor.

"Calling me kid again, huh?" Like the first day of training camp all those years ago.

She shrugs a shoulder as I walk backward onto the field. "Maybe I'll use your name if you get us to the Super Bowl."

"Just you wait, Frankie. Give me a minute to stop these guys, then I'm coming for you."

Houston lines up, calling their play.

"Newman, watch the tight end!" I shout to him, watching as they shift on the line.

The ball is hiked, and instead of their QB sneaking across the line, he passes it to the running back. I track his movement as he dodges left, then right, before deciding to go for it over the middle.

I meet his leap with one of my own, pushing his body back. I don't let up until the whistle blows and one of the guys is pulling me up.

Every single fan is going crazy cheering for us. Alex is running out onto the field, all business, as the team celebrates on the sideline.

We stopped them. We stopped Houston.

The Denver Mountain Lions are going to the Super Bowl.

The fucking Super Bowl.

"Way to finish, Knox!" Alex slaps me on the back as I run toward the sideline.

Frankie is clapping every guy on the helmet as they run past her, hugging her as they go.

Her eyes are wet when she finally sees me. Unlatching the strap under my helmet, I toss it toward the bench.

"Care to revisit that *kid*?" I quirk a brow at her.

"Guess I can call you Knox now that I know we're going to the Super Bowl."

"Hell yeah!"

She leaps into my arms, locking her ankles behind my back.

"That play was incredible the way you read him!" Pride drips from her words as I squeeze her to me.

"I learned from the best." I pull back, swiping a stray tear away.

Frankie was my first coach. Before we ever started this thing between us, she was the one teaching me to be a better player. I wouldn't be where I am today if it weren't for her.

Every player on the defense feels the same. Frankie is smart. She knows the game better than most of the coaches in the league.

To have her by my side as the final seconds wind down is special.

"Your Denver Mountain Lions are heading to the Super Bowl!" The announcer's voice echoes around the stadium.

"Holy shit! I can't believe it's happening!" Frankie peppers my face with kisses. "We're going to the Super Bowl, Knox!"

Brushing her hair aside, I take in her happiness. She's glowing, damn well bursting with pride.

"You got us here."

Frankie kisses me one last time, long and drugging, before sliding out of my arms.

"I love you." Frankie squeezes my hand.

"Not as much as I love you."

She rolls her eyes. "I doubt it."

"You going to argue with me?"

"You wouldn't love me if I didn't."

If that isn't the truth. Frankie is never one to back down from me. She pushes me in ways I never knew I needed. I'm a better man because of her. A better player. I hate to think about life without her.

Because it wouldn't be much of a life.

"Hell of a stop, Knoxy!" Colin jumps on my shoulders from behind. "Thanks for teaching our boy here, Frankie!"

"He did the hard work," Frankie says.

Never one to take the compliments.

She slips off to the other coaches as the guys crowd around me.

"We're going to the Super Bowl!" Alex says, confetti now mixing with the snow coming down onto the field.

"I can't believe it!" Jackson states, looking around the field. "We actually did it."

"It's been a long time coming," Logan agrees.

He's right. Even for him, coming in only a few years ago. We've all been in this league a long time. Most players will never make it to the big game, let alone win one.

To be here now, with these guys? I get choked up.

"There's no one else I'd rather be in this fight with than you guys," I say.

"Aww. Knox loves us." Colin is beside himself with excitement.

"He's always loved me," Logan says.

"Please. He loves me the most," Colin argues.

"Pretty sure it's Frankie he loves the most," Alex reminds them.

"Way to be the fun police, Alex." Colin rolls his eyes at him.

"I love each of you guys. I'll love you even more if you manage to bring home a Super Bowl for us."

Every set of eyes looks back at me. I look at the team celebrating around us as the stage is set to receive the AFC Championship trophy. I look at Frankie, now hugging my mom on the sideline.

It's nothing but pride and love for this group of guys. We busted our asses to get here. We played through pain and heartache to keep getting better every year.

Because while this win gets us one step closer, it's not the win we want. The one we want is in two weeks.

Two weeks to study and watch film.

Two weeks of nerves and pundits to speculate on if the Mountain Lions have what it takes to win the big game.

Two weeks.

That's all that stand between us and The Big Game.

Let's fucking go.

## THE END

Keep reading to see the story of how Knox and Frankie first hookup!

"Can I get another?" I wave the bartender down, needing another bourbon. That loss today was brutal. To add insult to injury, it was in the playoffs. And now we're stranded in Buffalo tonight because of the weather. Nothing like a foot of snow being dumped on a city celebrating their team's win and our loss.

A full glass of brown liquid is set down in front of me. I take a hearty swallow, relishing the burn.

"Trying to drown your sorrows?"

I turn toward the familiar voice. Frankie is there, half a beer in front of her.

"I could ask the same of you."

She moves down a seat, an empty stool sitting between us.

"After that loss? I'm surprised more of the team isn't down here."

I shake my head and swig down the rest of my drink. "Probably licking their wounds."

"Is destroying your liver the better option then?"

Frankie closes her lips around her beer bottle, taking a long pull.

"Hoping to forget that game. It fucking sucked."

"It wasn't your fault." Frankie's voice is matter-of-fact.

"It wasn't?" I quirk a brow in her direction. "That missed block at the end wasn't my fault?"

Frankie shakes her head. "It doesn't come down to one play. We didn't play our best football today. End of story."

"That's a fucking understatement." My tone is bitter. I can't help it. I'm pissed we lost. Another great season with nothing to show for it. "When is it going to happen for us?"

Frankie scoots over to the stool next to me. "It will. I know it will. We have one of the best teams." She grabs my arm, and immediately, a shock of electricity shoots through me. That's new. She must feel it too because she pulls back from me.

I don't know what comes over me, but it can only be the alcohol swirling in my veins that causes me to say, "Want to come back to my room with me?"

Frankie chokes over the sip she's taking as a blush creeps up her neck. She likes the idea.

"What the hell, Knox?"

I inch closer to her, and her dark pupils widen.

"Don't tell me you don't like the idea."

"I'm your coach."

"You don't have to be tonight."

"Knox…"

I can see her toying the idea around in her head. Now that I've said it out loud, I want her.

Fuck, do I ever want her. I've wanted her since the first day I walked onto the field with Roberts.

I finish my drink and set it on the bar with a clink. I don't miss the way she tracks my every move.

"Room five-seventeen. I'll wait an hour." I drop my mouth down by her ear. "Ball's in your hands, Frankie. Whatever decision you want to make is up to you."

I hear the slight intake of her breath.

I adjust myself in my joggers as I head to the elevators, saying a small prayer that she comes.

Because I want Frankie Rose.

Frankie

"CAN I GET YOU ANYTHING ELSE?" The bartender startles me out of my thoughts.

"No, thanks."

Unless it's a six-foot-one linebacker.

I drop a twenty onto the bar and head toward the elevator.

This is a bad idea. A really bad idea.

But one I have no doubt that I want to be a part of.

From that first day Knox walked onto the field, he's had a hold on me. In all the years I've been coaching, I've never felt the things I'm feeling for Knox.

Not only one of my players, but someone seven years younger than I am.

When the elevator opens to the fifth floor, it's quiet. After a long game, everyone wanted to go their own way.

I follow the signs to Knox's room. Finding the right door, I hesitate. If we do this, there's no going back.

All I can think about though was how dejected he looked earlier. It wasn't his fault. No one on the team played well.

Offense, defense, special teams. You name it, we all sucked today.

And right now, there's only one thing that can make me feel better.

Knox Fisher.

My knock is soft but it cuts through the quiet hallway like a bullet firing. Knox is at the door, opening it and pulling me inside.

The air is charged as I take him in like I never have before.

The Mountain Lions tee stretches over his chest, highlighting every one of his muscles. Tattoos swirl up and down his arm.

I can't wait to feel the scruff of his beard between my legs. The thought has me clenching my legs together.

"What are you thinking?" Knox tucks a lock of hair behind my ear. Up close, I can see the flecks of honey in his eyes.

I love how tall he is.

Being five-foot-nine myself, every man I was with before was always right at my height. It never bothered me in the past.

Not until right now.

Because I like that Knox looms large over me.

I want him to possess me. Dominate me. Command me in every way.

"I've coached dozens of players." I take a step closer to Knox, dropping my hands onto this chest.

Damn. I don't know if I've ever felt pecs that strong.

"Oh yeah?" Knox moves into my space, dragging his nose along my neck.

"I've never wanted any of them. But I want you. God help me, I want you."

Knox steals the breath from me as he crushes his lips to mine.

And oh, what a kiss it is.

I feel it everywhere. My toes curl as I dig my fingers into his chest. Each swipe of his tongue against mine has heat gathering between my legs.

A gasp escapes me as Knox backs me up against the wall. Hands fisting in my hair, he tilts my head to deepen the kiss.

*Oh God.*

How can this man be such a good kisser?

Knox's mouth moves down my jaw, nipping and kissing as he goes. My hips rock, seeking friction. Knox smirks against my jaw.

"Something wrong, Frankie?"

He pulls back. His eyes are filled with lust. No doubt they match my own.

"You know there is."

"And how can I help?" Knox drags a finger down the vein that throbs in my neck. He keeps moving it down my chest, hooking it into the V of my T-shirt.

Pushing myself off the wall, I walk us farther into the room. Knox has a cocky grin on his face. I don't care that I'm showing my need for him.

Knees hitting the bed, Knox pulls me onto his lap. He's rock hard beneath me.

*And huge.*

I lick my lips as I run my fingers through his thick hair. Knox's hands drift up and under my shirt. Hands that are rough from years of playing football.

Neither of us are making a move. We're taking each other in. A moment that feels almost inevitable.

Knox licks his lips as his eyes study me. Every thought

of why we shouldn't be doing this flees my head as I take his lips again.

It's hot as sin. Every swipe of my tongue against his has me growing wetter and wetter. I don't know how long I'll last once we finally get naked.

Because I want Knox more than anything.

Wrapping his arms around my waist, Knox flips us over and onto the bed. He presses his weight into me.

"Still time to back out, Frankie." His lips nip at my own. "If you don't want to do this, now's the time to say no."

Reaching for the bulge in his sweats, I squeeze his thick length. The muscles in his neck flex as I rub my palm over him. "There's still time if you want to back out," I parrot his words back to him.

Straddling my hips, Knox inches my shirt up over my chest. My breasts are heaving. No doubt my diamond-hard nipples are showing through my thin bra.

Something that Knox doesn't miss if his grin is anything to go by.

He leans down, sucking one into his mouth.

"Gah!" I lean into his touch. Holy shit, that feels good. He licks and sucks his way over to the other, showing it the same attention.

That mouth of his—the one that gives me so much trouble during practice—moves over the soft planes of my stomach. The closer he gets to my core, the tighter my need coils.

Knox pulls the band of my leggings down, nipping at my hip bone. I'm shameless in my wanton need. I want to feel that dick of his everywhere.

Sitting back on his heels, Knox pulls my leggings down my body. I take the opportunity to take off my shirt and bra, leaving me in only my cotton underwear. They're nothing sexy, but Knox doesn't seem to care.

"Fuck, you are gorgeous." His voice is gravelly as his eyes trail over me.

Gripping the back of his shirt, Knox pulls it off.

The man is built like a Greek god. Abs for days. A light dusting of chest hair.

Knox has a body that I want to climb like a tree.

My skin prickles at his lazy perusal. His eyes are greedily taking me in.

With Knox taking his time, I take matters into my own hands. Walking my fingers down my stomach, I slip them under the band of my underwear.

"What are you doing?" Knox tries to move my hand out of the way, but I swat his back.

"Someone needs to teach you—"

Knox scoffs. "I'm not some virgin, if that's what you're thinking."

Reaching up, I wrap a hand around Knox's neck and pull him down. Our foreheads touch as our breaths mingle. "I was going to say you haven't been with a woman like me. Someone needs to teach you how to please an older woman."

"Fuck, Frankie."

His eyes follow my body as I dip my fingers inside me. The heel of my hand brushes against my clit, already sensitive.

My fingers move in and out of me, just how I like. With Knox watching, it's driving me closer and closer to pleasure.

And he knows it.

Grabbing my hand, Knox pulls my hand out. His gaze is fixed on mine as he sucks my fingers into his mouth, swirling his tongue around the pads.

"How was that?" he asks as he takes my hand and drags it down his chest.

I shrug a shoulder. "C+."

"C+?" His voice is incredulous. We could spend the night making out, and I'd give him an A+. But he already has a big enough head. I don't need to make it any bigger.

I smile as I start to shove his pants down his thighs. "I guess that means you have a thing or two to learn."

Knox flops over on the bed, pushing his pants all the way down and kicking them off. His cock springs free.

Holy shit. He really is huge. It smacks him in his perfect abs, precum already leaking from the tip.

"Like something you see?" Knox gives himself a lazy stroke.

Stripping out of my underwear, I settle between his legs.

"Are you ready for your first lesson?"

"How is this you teaching me a lesson—" I cut him off by sucking the tip of him into my mouth.

The saltiness of him hits me right away. There's no way I'm going to be able to fit all of him inside, so I add my hand, stroking him as my tongue works him over.

"Fuck. That is so good."

I smile up at him as I continue my assault on him. He's leaking in my mouth. I don't know if Knox realizes that he's thrusting up into my mouth.

Driving him wild makes me get wetter. His hands find my hair, guiding me up and down his dick.

"Fuck. I could come just like this." His voice is laced with need. I pull off him with a pop.

"We can't have that now, can we?" I wipe my mouth.

Knox reaches down to the floor, no doubt looking for his wallet.

"Were your last test results negative?"

He nods.

"Mine too."

He understands the implication. "Are you sure?"

I stroke his slick cock. "Yes. I want to feel every inch of this inside of me."

"How are you real?" Knox leans up and takes my lips in a passionate kiss. He tastes like me and bourbon. It's intoxicating.

I push him back to the bed and take his dick in hand. Lining myself up, I sink down onto him.

"Yes," I hiss.

It feels so good. I can feel every ridge as he moves farther and farther inside of me. Knox's hands smooth down my back, clutching the globes of my ass. He holds me steady as he fully fills me.

"You feel fucking incredible," he breathes into my neck. "So fucking good, Frankie."

I plant my hands on either side of his head. "Not as good as you."

Knox squeezes, moving me ever so slightly over him. There's the slightest pinch of pain—no doubt from how he's stretching me.

I rock my hips, adjusting to the size. Knox takes a nipple between his teeth.

"Was that C+ material?"

I can't lie, not when I'm squeezing his cock to within an inch of its life. "Maybe a B-."

Knox slaps my ass. "Who knew you had such a mouth on you?"

I grin down at him as I shift my hips. The change in angle has him hitting a spot deep inside that no one has ever reached.

"Oh God."

"That's right. You know you like it."

Knox starts thrusting up as I move on top of him. We meet each other with each thrust. Knox's fingers find my clit, thrumming a steady rhythm over it.

It's sensory overload. My pleasure is at its tipping point. I want to hold back, but I can't. It's too much.

"Come on me, Frankie. I'm there."

He strums my clit one more time and it pushes me over the edge.

It's the orgasm to end all orgasms. I've never felt so much moving through me as Knox holds me to him as he spills his own release inside me. It's hot and messy and sweaty and fucking amazing.

"Holy shit," I whisper, collapsing against Knox.

"How was that?" His fingers trail down my spine.

I play with the chain that rests against his chest.

"B+," I jest.

"Damn, Frankie." Knox flips us over. "Guess I have to keep working for that A."

# Note from the Author

Book eleven is now out in the world!

Swoon…did I ever fall hard for Knox! I loved him from book one and it was so hard not to write his story right off the bat! I loved all the messages I got from readers about his book and wanting it! And the best part? WE STILL HAVE ONE MORE BOOK TO GO! The Mountain Lions are going to the Super Bowl!

To all the wonderful authors who I've met over the course of this journey…I wouldn't be here without you! I would've lost my mind ages ago, and I can't thank you enough for all your love and support!

To my street team, bookstagrammers and booktokers who have shared their love for this series…it seriously puts the biggest smile on my face! I can't tell you how happy it makes you that you love my guys as much as I do! To my reader group…I love hanging out with you guys!

And to all you readers who have picked up my books… thank you for taking a chance on my books. You're the best part of this journey for me!

<3 Emily

# About the Author

After winning a Young Author's Award in second grade, Emily Silver was destined to be a writer. She loves writing strong heroines and the swoony men who fall for them.

A lover of all things romance, Emily started writing books set in her favorite places around the world. As an avid traveler, she's been to all seven continents and sailed around the globe.

When she's not writing, Emily can be found sipping cocktails on her porch, reading all the romance she can get her hands on and planning her next big adventure!

Find her on social media to stay up to date on all her adventures and upcoming releases!